I0762068

Goose River Anthology, 2011

Edited by

Deborah J. Benner

Goose River Press
Waldoboro, Maine

Library of Congress Card Number: 2011932852.

ISBN: 978-1-59713-110-0

First Printing, 2011

Cover photo by Caron Tanguay.

Published by
Goose River Press
3400 Friendship Road
Waldoboro ME 04572
gooseriverpress@roadrunner.com
www.gooseriverpress.com

Table of Contents

Table of Contents

Table of Contents

Table of Contents

Table of Contents

Dedicated to my children,
Marcus & Kasey

and in memory of my Sheba

Juliana L'Heureux
Topsham, ME

Vietnam War Memories

Our Jetstar flight from Singapore into Ho Chi Minh City began a week long visit filled with historic memories. My husband, a Vietnam War Veteran, and I landed at the new Tan Son Nhat International Airport in Ho Chi Minh City. Our guide named Ban (Vietnamese for "Ben") met us at the airport. He pointed out an old airplane terminal, the last building remaining of the original air base, which was a familiar name used during the 1960's - 70's Vietnam War. It was the Tan Son Nhat Air Base.

During the war, the air base was a place where bad news streamed ticker tape reports of body counts. It was where many journalists filed their news stories when they covered the unpopular Vietnam War.

My memory quickly blocked the flag-draped coffins we often saw on the runway during those newscasts.

Those soldiers in the flag draped coffins are now among the 58,267 names, carved on the reflective black granite wall on the Vietnam War Memorial in Washington DC.

Today, Vietnam War memories are secondary to the ambitious Vietnamese people. They are proud of their united country and working toward a prosperous economy. Mostly, it's only the older generation who call Ho Chi Minh City by its old capital name of Saigon.

My husband, Richard, was with the US Navy Seabees Mobile Construction Batallion 71 (MCB-71) when he served in Vietnam in 1967 and with the air craft carrier, *USS Intrepid* CVS-11, in the Golf of Tonkin, in 1969.

Our visit to Vietnam, beginning with Tan Son Nhat Air Base, started a memory walk into our family's Vietnam War history.

Our memories are not exclusively about two Vietnam deployments with the Navy. During our years as a Navy fam-

Juliana L'Heureux
Topsham, ME

ily, we were involved with the air lift of refugees from Saigon, beginning on April 30, 1975, when the city fell to the North Vietnamese. At that time, our family lived in Subic Bay in the Philippines where we helped the International Red Cross to receive and process the numerous waves of refugees who were evacuated by air from the US Embassy during the fall of Saigon and flown to Subic Bay.

Today, the iconic site where the US helicopter lifted off the roof of the US Embassy in Saigon is now the American Consulate. A new embassy is located in Hanoi, the capital city of the reunited Vietnam.

We visited the site of the US Consulate while in Ho Chi Minh City, where we saw a line of about 50 people who gathered there daily to wait for appointments they hoped would help them to immigrate to the US. Our attempts to take photographs of the Consulate were waved off by the security guards.

My husband commented about his days in Vietnam during our first night in Ho Chi Minh City. Certainly, the modern Grand Hotel in downtown Saigon was a lot different than his life on a Seabee base in a war zone. He said it was the first time he was in Vietnam without hearing gun fire.

Nonetheless, the experience of gun fire became real again when our guide drove us to visit the site of the Cu Chi Tunnels, about one hour outside of Ho Chi Minh City. The Cu Chi Tunnel Historic Site was once the secret operational base of the Liberated Zone occupied by the Viet Cong. Cruel primitive traps used by the Viet Cong army to inflict pain on people were displayed and demonstrated by guides during the tunnel tour. Other working exhibits along the dirt path in and out of the site demonstrated how the Viet Cong Army lived during the war years.

Particularly difficult to watch were the demonstrations of the booby traps used by the Viet Cong to injure and capture American and Vietnamese soldiers, who became snarled in lethal contraptions disguised as jungle foliage.

Juliana L'Heureux
Topsham, ME

Even more startling, as the tour progressed, were the sounds of M16 rifle fire we heard during the one hour walking tour in jungle terrain.

Believe it or not, the gun fire sound effects were intentional, creating a sense of uncertainty, because they were happening close to the walking exhibits. It turned out (we discovered by asking) that, for a small fee, visitors were allowed to fire American M16 rifles in a nearby gun quarry. In fact, the experience of hearing gun fire gave us the feeling of being in a jungle war zone.

Indeed, a retro moment, a fleeting flashback swept through my husband as we witnessed events in the exhibit that, in fact, killed Americans and Vietnamese. These killing events happened on a daily basis when my husband's war routines were filled with the sounds of gunfire.

"Well! So much for remembering Vietnam without gunfire," I said.

Our immersion into the Cu Chi Tunnels became surreal as we progressed. We felt the war, as though it might resurrect itself. We wanted to get through the walking tour as soon as possible.

Awful looking war relics were untouched as they remained on the jungle paths, left behind by the Vietnamese Liberation Army (i.e., Viet Cong) for future generations to witness. Among these were the charred remains of a US Army tank that was attacked while, presumably, trying to destroy the tunnels. Jungle growth was shading the huge bomb craters made by B52 fighter planes; the impacts of those aerial assaults were evident where giant sunken holes marked the bombs' targets. War armament exhibits were displayed adjacent to a few of the B52 crater holes.

Our hike through the humidity of the Vietnam jungle, walking the same trails we likely watched as young adults on a televised war, was like opening a coffin to view the remains. We wanted to see it, but our experience was not a rewarding one. We know Americans and Vietnamese lost their lives because of the Cu Chi Tunnels. We know Americans died and lost the war to the Vietnamese Liberation Army.

Difficult war memories notwithstanding, we made a point to walk the streets of Ho Chi Minh City. We recommend the delicious Asian cuisine, as all the restaurants served excellent food. In spite of streets heavily congested with motor bikes, we walked to places where colonial French culture and architecture are still evident. Old buildings like the Saigon post office were built during the 100 years when the country was part of France's empire in South East Asia. It's a great place to buy reasonably priced souviners.

Saigon's Notre Dame Basilica, built by the French in 1880, is located downtown across the street from the Post Office.

We were delighted to find a familiar artifact. Several 60 pound large ceramic elephants adorned the religious shrines to Saint Joan d'Arc and the Vietnamese Martyrs inside the Bascilica. We particularly enjoyed finding the elephants because we happen to have several just like them. They are ceramic relics of the Vietnam War years, when servicemen looked to take something home. Many veterans sent the large elephants home with their personal effects, especially if they could be loaded on Navy ships for transport back to the US.

Few people we spoke with took the time to mourn the loss of South Vietnam's civil war with the north, on April 30, 1975. Ben said his family was required to attend the Vietnam government's brain washing rehabilitation camps following the war.

Vietnamese people seemed to be enthusiastic about their future. There was no evident animosity towards Americans in South Vietnam because of the loss of the war, at least, not as far as we could see.

American dollars ruled the economy. In fact, Vietnam currency, i.e., the Dong, was practically worthless while we were there. Many commercial transactions asked for American dollars. Even our entry into the country required

Juliana L'Heureux
Topsham, ME

$25 US for each Visa presented at the time of arrival. No credit cards, no checks, only US cash. We wondered what a Russian or European visitor thought about needing US dollars to enter Vietnam.

As we flew out of Vietnam, I never bothered to look for the old Tan Son Nhat airplane terminal during our departure. It's an old building soon to be consumed in a landscape of the modern Vietnam, one bustling with the sounds of new construction and economic optimism.

***

Sally Belenardo
Branford, CT

Spring Song of Chickadee

The lungs of March inhale
what's left of snow
and somewhere always distant
a small bird's invisible voice appears—
a frail, sighing whistle,
descending phrase of two syllables
clear through the air

calling back
the breath-taking joy
of the first warmer day
in my childhood years—

evoking an age-old sorrow:
The song the same, and life so changed.

Dianisha Leonard
Worcester, MA

Leaving

While she sits by her bedside,
the light from the moon shines through the window.
Tears of regret trickle down her face,
as she thinks of days gone by.
Not able to change what has already been done,
she slowly drifts deep into sleep.
So vivid and real are the images behind her eyes,
the smiling face that she no longer knows.
What has become of this person?
No longer does she revel in the sound of the wind,
nor the pleasant chirping of birds at her window.
So bleak everything looks now.
Such radiant light and vibrant color,
have now turned to pale shades of gray.
Her eyelids flutter as she slips into oblivion,
her presence a mere memory.
As a small spark still flickers,
a glimmer of hope,
she smiles contently before leaving.

***

Sally Belenardo
Branford, CT

Gardener's Guide

Cultivate the soil.
Sow, fertilize and water.
Then weed it and reap.

Sherry B. Hanson
Brunswick, ME

Philips Cemetery, Erie PA

Eighteen miles east of Erie
on interstate 90 lies Philips Cemetery
gracing a rise opposite
Kwik Fill truck stop.

The lake stretches emerald green,
July breeze off the water
tosses branches of cedar and spruce,
pink clover cascades the banking.

Ghosts are probably out and about
eyeing marigolds at this grave,
sniffing petunias around that stone,
waving small flags for the veterans
and a mariner gone down with his ship.

Summer's warm wind is kind
teasing the sumac, shaking the aspen,
ricocheting among ghosts and
glancing off headstones
until November gales
drive every living thing to ground.

sarah p. roy
Oakland, ME

Requiem

for an old barn falling into dust,
settles amid tangled grass,
bones layered deep
a sheltered ground to seek.

Lupines intermingle
with daisies,
buttercups,
Indian paintbrushes—

red
yellow
white
purple

a box of crayons strewn
with shadows of gray
bring out a final
sense of beauty

and

loss.

Rosemarie Nervelle
Camden, ME

Ethel and Bertie

Ethel and Bertie had coffee at Al's Diner every Sunday morning after Mass. It was a habit they eased into after Ethel's husband died. The hour or so they spent discussing certain members of their congregation provided Bertie a pleasant distraction from her everlasting duty: visiting her mentally handicapped son in the county home every Sunday afternoon.

No longer invited to gatherings for "couples," Ethel missed her social life more than her departed husband. Ethel and Bertie had lived in the same small town all their lives. They attended the only Catholic Church in town, but never formally approached one another. Bertie was always one of the women in the kitchen who made the coffee, put out the sandwiches and cut the cakes. By the time she and others of her ilk had cleaned up, all the affluent and sophisticated ladies had made their social plans for the coming week and left, except Ethel. Desperate for someone, anyone, and for any reason to delay her return to an empty house on Sunday mornings, she latched on to Bertie's invitation.

Ethel wasn't especially fond of Bertie, but she was the only woman who had spoken kindly to the new widow from the pass-through of the church kitchen. Bertie didn't seem a bit jealous of Ethel's obvious charms. Unlike many of the other senior women in the congregation, Bertie had no husband for Ethel to flirt with. Consequently, Bertie thought a friendship with Ethel might prove interesting, giving her the opportunity for a prestigious friendship from the other side of town.

At the beginning of their casual friendship, Bertie divulged her sixty-eight years in an attempt at closeness, while Ethel voiced a half-hearted compliment that Bertie didn't appear to be "looking down the throat of seventy." Bertie

Rosemarie Nervelle
Camden, ME

was suspicious of Ethel's reluctance to confess her age, and often made references to events that took place "before Ethel's time," attempting to catch her in a time-sequence blunder. Ethel indulged her friend in her "age-discovery" game, confident that Bertie wouldn't catch her off-guard.

After all was said and done, Ethel did look younger. Her husband had left her financially comfortable. Ethel Dandridge-Smith was still quite attractive, wore make-up, and had her beehive hair-do and nails done every week. She shopped at specialty stores for her clothes and dressed in appropriate styles.

Bertie, on the other hand, had been early widowed; a domestic worker all her life. She spent a lot of time looking for "almost-new" clothing at the local second-hand store. Years of responsibility for her handicapped son had long ago sucked the youth from her face.

Ethel sat at the table opposite Bertie, her hands folded under a chin that was beginning to show "banjo strings." She manipulated her manicured fingers so that the sun sparkled off her diamond rings. She looked around the diner with displeasure, then forced a weak smile to secretly encourage those customers whom she caught admiring her comportment.

"I meant to ask you before, Bertie, wouldn't you rather have coffee at a nicer, more genteel coffee house?"

"I don't see nothin' wrong with Al's place," Bertie replied, dunking her donut. Been comin' here for years. I like the folks, and the coffee's good. I remember when Al's family opened this diner. I think it was in the forties, wasn't it?"

"I wouldn't know," Ethel replied, turning away from Bertie's eyes. "That was before my time."

Ethel looked around at the caliber of people who frequented the diner. Many of Al's customers were down on their luck, their shoulders hunched over a bowl of soup, eyeing the homemade donuts piled in a sugary pyramid under a plastic dome on the counter. Al stood behind flipping pancakes, scrambling eggs and frying bacon, wiping his hands on yesterday's apron.

"Really, Bertie. Look at the filthy rag he's wearing. Aren't people who prepare food in restaurants supposed to wear nets, or caps; something to cover their hair. Every time he flips a pancake I can almost see flakes of dandruff fall into the batter. Oh, my!" She groaned and dropped her head into her hands.

"I don't know nothin' about that, Ethel. Al's as clean as the next guy. I remember comin' here as a kid with my folks. Al's dad was runnin' it then. Al and his family worked here right through the Depression; fed a lot of folks who couldn't afford even a bowl of soup once a day. Nobody worried about a few flakes of dandruff, or even a mouse turd when they found one on their plate." Bertie rolled her eyes at Ethel who seemed to cringe from even thinking about such things.

Ethel turned away in disgust, pushing the plate with her untouched donut toward Bertie.

Bertie smiled and waved to Al when he slid a heaping plate of steaming pancakes on the counter in front of a customer. Al waved back, again wiping his hands on his apron, and came around the counter to their table.

"Hi, Bertie. How's tricks?" Al asked good-naturedly, patting his gray comb-over into place.

"I'm just fine, Al. Don't see you around here much any more."

"I just opened another place in the next county. Been tryin' to get it together before the season starts. I'm cookin' here for a few days 'cause my nephew Joey took sick with appendix."

Al turned to Ethel and smiled. "Who's your friend, Bertie?"

"Oh, sorry, Al. This here is Ethel Dandridge-Smith."

Al said, "Pleased to meet ya, Ethel," holding out his still-damp hand. Ethel took it as if it were the head of a dead snake.

Rosemarie Nervelle
Camden, ME

"How do you do," said Ethel, wiping her offended hand on her napkin.

Al noticed, the smile quickly vanishing from his face.

"Don't I know you from somewhere? You look familiar. I remember a Dandridge family who lived a few doors down from here, thirty—forty years ago. You one of them?"

"I think not," Ethel answered curtly. Something about this man made her uncomfortable.

"Ethel don't go back that far, Al. Couldn't be the same family." Bertie felt the excitement of Ethel's impending come-uppance crawl up her fleshy arms. Enjoying the exchange of information on old friends with Bertie, Al closely scrutinized Ethel until she began to squirm on her chair.

"Wait a second!" he suddenly exclaimed. "I do know you!" Al tapped a finger to his temple. "Yeah, sure, I graduated from high school with an Ethel Dandridge in 1942.

"Yeah. Threw me over, you did, for Buster Smith. Married him right after graduation. I heard he'd died. Too bad. I liked Buster. He was a great guy."

Someone called from behind the counter. "Good seein' you, Bertie. Take care."

Grinning from ear to ear, Al waved and called over his shoulder as he disappeared through the kitchen door, "You're lookin' pretty good for your age, Ethel. See you around."

Anne Hammond
Woolwich, ME

White Tip

Dropped by the glacier long ago,
The boulder solos in the middle of the bay,
Granite shoulders splashed orange with lichen,
Tide line a rim of rockweed.
Never long deserted,
The megalith gathers populations of gull and cormorant
When high tides cover the ledges nearer to the sea.

Flocks of migrating plover arrive one September day
To tuck their heads, lift one leg, and rest.
A great blue heron does not disturb them
When it settles with ponderous flaps on top of the rock
In the notch inhabited by a tuft of grass
Where earlier in the season a pair of terns built a nest
And fledged their young.

Snowy egrets share the lithoid perch
Nubbled with facets of feldspar and patches of quartz.
Isolated by expanses of mud at low tide
And deep water during times of flood,
White Tip is not merely a bedrock boulder
Birthed in the heart of the earth,
But a refuge signaling safety and survival.

Tom Crowley
Lincolnville, ME

A Bad Tide at Owls Head

Last night we had a bad tide
Come to Owls Head Bay
It brought bad news, too
But we had to stay.

This is our home
And this is our life
It's long and its hard
Like a baitfish knife.

They sunk three boats
And left them to drop
Deep in the harbor
To make us stop.

No man should do that
No man I ever knew
But these were not men
They were cowards and few.

We will rise up
And our boats will rise too.
We will fish again
Though the lobsters are few.

This is our home
And we all share the sea
There's few things we don't share
Like grief over tea.

Tom Crowley
Lincolnville, ME

Deb had a bake for us Sunday
At the Ship to Shore.
A lot of folks came
We thank all for sure.

But Monday came fast
And three men had to wait
As they caulked in the dawn
To seal boats and their fate.

This is our home
And this is our way
We will fish again
God will bring a new day.

***

Karen Lewis Foley
Topsham, ME

Dragonfly

On the bleached porch rail
the thick black body
tethers its length on tense legs,
round robot head weaving the air.

Four unfeathered wings
throw naked sparkles,
shudder in the wind
like grounded kites.

Jeannie E. Roberts
Chippewa Falls, WI

Rush River Valley

Just before sunrise,
encircled by air, thick
with the dampness
of summer, heavy

with the fragrance
of earth, quiet
with predawn's pulse,
before monarchs glide

and meadowlarks whistle,
I walk this dappled field;
through yarrow, aster,
milkweed—past thistle,

by spiking Oswego tea,
where light awakens
this valley, awakens me.
In this place, flowing

before lobelia, beside
flood-beaten banks, coursing
below limestone cliffs,
waters rush south

to meet Lake Pepin.
Surging through me
renewal rises, in this
my Rush River Valley.

Janet Morgan
Wiscasset, ME

Girl Scout Jamboree, or the Disaster of 1959

"Get up, get up now!" My mother sounded angry, but this could not be. She never got angry. Was I dreaming? No such luck. The truth is that this was not the first time she had called me, which might explain why her voice held a rare sign of impatience. In all honesty, this had to have been about the tenth time she had told me to get up. This, I finally realized, as the fog lifted.

I opened one eye. It was the ungodly hour of—I had no idea what—but it was way before dawn. So why was she about to pull the covers off my bed? And then the light dawned, not from outside my darkened window, but from inside my head: the Girl Scout Jamboree!

Now I don't even know if the Girl Scouts have a jamboree, but we were going on the closest thing to one that I'll ever experience. With this in mind, I jumped out of bed, threw on my clothes, grabbed my backpack, and I was ready! It was my cousin Dea who had talked me into this camping trip. I was a Girl Scout, but I didn't have nearly as many badges as Dea. She told me that if I went, I would get at least one new scout badge. Lord knows I needed a few more. My sash hung around my neck unadorned. It held so few badges that it shamed me to wear it. It was pitiful. I had but two badges: one for completing some now forgotten craft and the other—thanks to my father—for sighting and identifying the minimum number birds necessary to earn the badge in question.

But, before I could think of a protest to this foolhardy outing, it was time to go. I dragged my backpack behind me as I all but crawled into the car with my mother. By the time we had picked up Dea, there wasn't any room left in the car. Dea had brought a tent and camping supplies her brother Gary had provided. I had my books. She looked at me as if I was out of my tree when she spied my contribution, but Mom

Janet Morgan
Wiscasset, ME

saved the day. She had packed all my gear in the trunk the night before because she knew that, to my mind, a backpack filled with books was all I needed.

When we met up with the troop on the school grounds, I was pleased to spy some like minded girls—for they, too, appeared less than happy—among an otherwise enthusiastic bunch of kids. Again, my thoughts of protest were not given time to be voiced before we were hustled into a school bus like a herd of cattle off to the slaughter. And we were off. Several pickup trucks had also been commandeered to deposit our gear near the foot of Mount Hunger. It was too late to retreat. I must make the best of the situation. We were being transported away from all we knew and there would be no chance of return until we had done what we had been sent away to do.

The bus rolled down through town and over a bridge before turning onto a side road with the trucks following along behind us. The cavalcade went on and on. It seemed to take forever for us to reach our destination. *Would the sun never come up,* I wondered, *or would we be hiking in the dark?* This was one fear I needn't have worried about, for the sun just peeked over the horizon as the vehicles came to a stop.

By this time I had learned that we would be hiking to a spot about halfway up the mountain. Looking around, I asked myself an important question: *Who's taking all this stuff up that mountain? And why was I here?* It was all Dea's fault! Last year Gary had gone on a jamboree, a real Boy Scout Jamboree. He returned from New York with all sorts of stories to tell about his adventures. And now it was supposed to be our turn! But do girls get to go on exciting trips to far-away places? No, we were headed for a tenting week on a mountain in Edgecomb, Maine. We were less than ten miles from home.

And I soon found out who would be carrying all that gear: we would. Packed down with so much stuff I knew my back

Janet Morgan
Wiscasset, ME

would break before we reached the top, I trudged along. Are we having fun yet? I grumbled under my breath. It looked as if some girls were, or perhaps those were just grimaces on their faces. When I looked over at Dea, she broke out in a real smile. Apparently she was having fun. It seemed to take hours for us to reach the clearing where we would be spending a whole week. In reality, it took much less time to hike to our destination—and that was a good thing—because we weren't done yet.

"Okay, drop your stuff where you want to place your tent and let's go," the troop leader announced. *Where are we going?* I thought. I soon learned. We were going back down the hill, again and again. We brought up load after load, until we were all ready to drop. I have to admit, however, that once we were up there and sitting on our mountainous packs, it was beautiful!

I can live with this, I thought—for about half a minute. "Time to set up camp now," our scout leader clapped her hands with too much gusto. "Everyone put up your tents, get your gear inside, and meet me in the center of the campground for assignments," she announced. *Assignments! We aren't in school. This is summer,* I wanted to say, but I was wise enough to keep my mouth shut.

Dea looked just as nonplussed as I was as we began to assemble Gary's tent. It wasn't a very big tent, so it should have been easy to get it up. It wasn't. "What's wrong with this thing? It won't go up like Gary showed me," Dea complained. I sat in frustration as I observed other girls erecting their tents with ease. But a few others needed help, too, and our scout leader obliged by coming to the rescue of anyone who was having trouble. When our tent rose majestically towards the blue sky, we sighed and entered.

This did not last long, however, for as soon as we had all our gear inside, we were ferreted out for those promised assignments. We couldn't hide from our over-eager leader. Most of us got latrine duty. As I wondered if we would be

Janet Morgan
Wiscasset, ME

expected to dig a trench with our fingers, Dea pulled two collapsible shovels from her pack. She handed me one. *Gee, thanks,* I thought as we headed for the designated spot. Some kids got to dig the barbecue pits, which seemed much more desirable, considering what they would soon be used for.

Tired, dirty, and sweaty, Dea and I finally dragged ourselves towards what we would laughingly be calling home for the next seven days. I could see other kids doing the same thing, so I didn't feel too bad about it. But no, the scout leader said we weren't done. "Firewood, you have to collect branches and larger pieces of wood if you want to eat. Everyone get out there and forage!" She yelled and we jumped.

So, okay, once the chores were done, the first day was fun. We all sat around a campfire and ate together as we chatted. After dark, we all gathered around the fire again for a songfest and spooky stories. But you try to get to sleep with owls hooting and the wind rustling the tree branches after that! I tossed and turned, but Dea was soon snoring. That simple noise sounded surprisingly peaceful. Eventually I did doze off, only to find we were expected to get up with the birds.

Our second day was filled with adventure. We did more chores, true, but we also took nature hikes; we identified birds and other wildlife on the mountain. During those hikes, we also learned a few simple woodland crafts. I earned a couple more cherished badges along the way, so life was good. That part was fun, but I never did get to read any of my books during those first days. The next day proved to be much like the first ones, but that bucolic feeling was not to last.

On the fourth day—after three beautifully sunny days—the rains began. The skies opened up and beat down upon us. The one good thing about it was that we were allowed to stay inside our tents and entertain ourselves. Now my books

Janet Morgan
Wiscasset, ME

became useful. This was heavenly, all but when I had to visit the latrine. The trenches eventually turned into muddy slides of revulsion.

As for the meals, we were fortunate to have adults with us. I, for one, didn't feel bad about not knowing how to light a fire in the rain. None of the other girls could, either, but the troop leader and her assistants soon had a blazing fire going. Of course, the food got soggy before we could eat it, but it still tasted heavenly.

By the fifth day, we were faced with a torrential downpour of biblical proportions. When it failed to abate, I looked at Dea as we sat in our soggy tents and said, "I bet you're glad now that I brought all these books!" She just sighed, picked out another book, and tried—with little success—to find a dry place to sit and read.

When the rain began flowing into the campsite, even the adults didn't bother with trying to light a campfire. This is when we learned what our emergency packs were for. Dry crackers with peanut butter washed down with water became the norm.

It wasn't long before Dea and I had opened our last remaining cold packs of food. Everything was getting wet. The only semi-dry spot was atop the wooden boxes each of us had been given. Dea and I sat huddled on them with our feet tucked beneath us. We kept praying for the rain to stop, until we heard the sweetest words ever spoken: "Abandon ship! Take only necessities!"

I picked up my books and shoved them into my pack. I was ready! I didn't have to be told twice. I was sick of the whole thing. But this abandonment turned out to be only an option. We could stay if we wanted to. And a few girls—those with dozens of merit badges and an attitude—huddled together in their tents and refused to leave. I had ungracious thoughts: *Let them drown. I'm going home, now!* I know I was being selfish, but I no longer cared. Let them have all the scout badges. And I guess they deserved them for their fool-

Janet Morgan
Wiscasset, ME

hardy bravery. I no longer cared.

Most of the tents stood abandoned and forlorn as we left camp behind. Dressed in our yellow slickers, we slogged down the hill in rubber boots. Our feet squelched and almost disappeared into the mud, but we didn't care, even as the mud threatened to suck our boots off our feet. We were headed back to civilization. We will return was the motto some kids uttered, as we were loaded onto the waiting bus. *I wasn't coming back,* I vowed. Anyway, I thought with ingratitude, *it was Gary's tent.*

***

e. w. oestreich
Damariscotta, ME

No Proper Place

There is no proper place to prop
the stone
with heavy weight to stop the closing
of the door. An evening breeze precedes the
night and puts an end to light.

But mourning doves who feed
at dawn
set quietly the door ajar—and blue of
morning light flew in
the opening

and tempts our hesitant and timid
feet to go outdoors again and play . . .

Mollie Schmidt
Rome, ME

Storm

Waves paw at the gravel shore,
low thunder over western hill
sounds like someone moving
cargo around the hold of a ship;

the air is electric, rainbrown,
holding its breath before the first
drops, then patter, then deluge
of cloud-sent, wind-fanned wet—

an enormous cell above, dark gray
that ponders across the lakesky,
throwing darts indiscriminately
to lighten the gloom for an instant;

blossoms bounce in the onslaught,
roots lap revivifying seepage—
where is my umbrella?
The cat wants to come in.

F. Anthony D'Alessandro
Orlando, FL

Sibling Celebration

The home plate sized and gooey, ebony cake announced,
"Happy Bicentennial Bill and Dot?"
Gnarled fingers interlocked in a loving hand lock.
Clamped to her nonagenarian baby brother like a human vice,
big sister tugged him toward her, repeating a rehearsed scene from Flapper times.
He turned away looking like the ripest Macintosh Apple.

Frowning and curling her brow at his "cool" body language,
she yanked his arms in like an obstinate horse's reins.
Was this to be the final squeeze for the surviving, wrinkled grapes on the December vine?
An invisible, silent communication oozed between the twin set of clouded eyes.
Their stares excluded all others from their private recital,
in this, the winter of their collective near two century marathon.

Four generations spilled out of the palm-lined party room surrounding them.
Laughter exploded and off color jokes proliferated.
Children screeched, babies bawled, and parents chastised.
Meaningless football images sauntered across the scratchy screen.

None of that traffic detoured the seasoned soul mates.
Their arms linked, minds united, in a run-on replay of youth.
Big sister framed little brother's face inside her crinkled bony hand,

(continued)

F. Anthony D'Alessandro
Orlando, FL

and softly pressed her lips to his nose.
Oblivious to the cratered curse squatting on their faces,
oblivious to runaway teeth,
oblivious to detoured tales trapped within the cavernous earwax, they cuddled, silently reflecting on their shared lives.

Interloping music racketed.
Finally, they unwrapped, defying rusted bodies, and they stiffly stood.
Heads up and proud they shared their ultimate shuffle, a staccato sputtering Irish Jig, while preparing for a looming reunion in Killarney's patch of Paradise.
The rude and disrespectful banditry of age failed to snatch or even detour their effervescent spirits.

***

P. C. Moorehead
North Lake, WI

A Tree

A tree...life.
The warmth of the sun penetrating its branches...love.
Blessed are we who have life and love.
Good it is that we are here.

P. C. Moorehead
North Lake, WI

Life's Coin

"How to measure value?" we ask.
"Is it the silver cast,
the solid depth,
the engraving so precise?"

"It is all of these and more," Life answers.
"It is the wisdom of our experience,
the acceptance of our suffering,
the joy of our transformation."

"We are life's coin,
precisely engraved,
enduring in love,
measured in value of giving."

***

Scrunching

The table has a leaf in it.
I take it out,
and scrunch the halves
together.

So it is with me.
I take out the unneeded,
scrunch together what is left
and form a whole
for the feast.

Joan Grant
Round Pond, ME

Seeing-Eye Brother

Tables and chairs were arranged in rows facing a grand piano in the elegant lobby of the Eastland Hotel in Portland. The occasion was a student recital which was part of the annual International Piano Festival.

The room was filling quickly so I got a complimentary cup of coffee, found an empty table and slid my wet umbrella under the chair. Off to my right I noticed an old man sitting on a lone chair that faced the audience. He didn't look like a concert-goer but this piano recital was free so I figured he perhaps just wandered into the hotel lobby to get out of the rain.

The man didn't seem down-and-out like most of the homeless who hang out in the nearby park. He wasn't disheveled. Perhaps I was wrong to judge him by his plaid shirt, rumpled khaki pants and worn blue baseball cap that he kept on through the whole event. But he certainly was different from the other people who were attending the piano recital.

He saw me looking at him from across the room and the eye contact must have emboldened him

"It's good to listen to music," he shouted as a conversation starter.

I nodded in agreement and mumbled, "Yes."

"Music calms you down," he added in his loud voice. I took a harder look at him to see if he needed "calming down."

"If it wasn't for my older brother, I never would have listened to music," he went on. "My brother is blind and my whole life I had to be his seeing-eye dog. So I took him to things he could hear...concerts, opera, symphonies. I've been to so many. I love music and I never would have heard any except for my brother."

The recital began and he sat rapt as the young pianists

Joan Grant
Round Pond, ME

played. He applauded enthusiastically after each performance.

When the concert ended he walked towards me leaning heavily on his handmade walking stick. It was probably carved out of a root as the handle part twisted in an odd series of curves and the bottom spread out into three branches that gripped the ground firmly.

"This was great. I came to hear the Khachaturian but the Chopin was good too. I hadn't heard Chopin before," he said.

"I listen to music alone now. My brother's not here," he said as we went from the warm lobby into the cold, stormy street.

The man headed up High Street and I opened my umbrella and walked in the opposite direction. The sound of the pelting rain reminded me of the cadence of the music we had just heard, but it was drowned out by thoughts of the old man hobbling up the hill.

Fortunate fellow. He learned to hear because his brother couldn't see.

Liz Moser
Phippsburg, ME & Baltimore, MD

Work in Progress

The sandcastle
follows a dreambuilt blueprint
conceived two lives ago
to the most exact detail.

It stands, spires reaching to the sun,
yet requires
constant shoring up,
story after story,
windows, ledges, doors holding
open lips from early kisses, handheld walks through cedar
woods,
moonlit bedclothes, hungry arms and legs

always needing care,
remolding corners
blunted by wind, weather, time and careless touches;
redefining boundaries
between the structure proper
and the beach
anonymous and open

year in year out.

Today the spires gleam
in celebration.

Tomorrow, maybe
only memories
in sandgrains
near incoming tide.....

Hannah Fox Trowbridge
Harpswell, ME

I'm Not Here Anymore, Mom

I know what you say is true, Susan.
You are not here anymore. But
I liked drinking out of the coffee cup
with your name on it. I bought it
for you in Florida; it helped me to touch you.

Until the handle broke off three successive times
after I glued it.

I wondered if that was your way
to tell me, "Let go of me, Mom."
Maybe I didn't respect your life
and death journey as your own to keep sacred.
I kept you here by touching your things.
But you are not here anymore.

It is your journey. I haven't completely let
you have it. Not really, like when I hold your cup, your clothes,
set up your shrines throughout the house,
and touch your stuffed animals, your sheets and blankets
because you slept on them.

I "mind talk" to you, ask you questions.
You "answer" me from your wisdom place.
I am here in my earth place. My heart hurts.
I'll try to honor your plan now,
if you'll guide me patiently.

Hannah Fox Trowbridge
Harpswell, ME

I am your mom here and love you there
maybe even more than when you were here.
You teach me how to love better than I did before.
You teach me the knowing you knew so well here
and that you now know even better there.

My soul still yearns to be with you.

"It's not about forgetting me, Mom.
You won't, I know.
You won't, you know.
It's about letting me go."

***

Karen Lewis Foley
Topsham, ME

Laura's Climb

Rising through wind and perfect branches
she comes to the most perfect and
to stillness in the midst of stained-glass
green leaves and apricots.

To the left the azure mountains drift
above California in the mist
that creeps up their sides
from the valley where she lives.

To the right oh! shining heads rise high
in the neighbor's field! The sunflowers
engolden her vision, dip and dance in the wind.
They slowly turn all day, following the sun.

Karen Loeb
Eau Claire, WI

Alberto in the Carport

From the sounds of it
your engine is about to up
and die. I live right next
door—me and the missus
heard all the commotion
what with you revving the
gas pedal to hold the
connection. If you'd like, I'll
take a look-see under the hood.
Can't hurt to take a peek
but to be honest, it don't
sound good. I'll adjust the
timing—now give it a try.
What you got here is a bunch
of gunk somewhere in a line
a regular convention of
ooze and slime. Don't
worry, there's a cure: Marvel's
Mystery Oil. I've got some
in my garage. Hold on—
just a few drops should do her.
Go ahead and turn the key. Does
this stuff work, or does this stuff work?

Robert Erickson
Round Pond, ME

A Piano Like Portland

Portland, Maine is an old port town located about a hundred miles northeast of Boston. It was in it's glory during the whaling period of New England history when the tall masted sailing ships set sail around the horn bound for the prolific whaling waters off San Francisco and Alaska, filling their holds with the oil that lighted the lamps of the western world. The ships sailed for years at a time, many carrying the whale oil to the far eastern ports of China and Malaysia, returning with the spices of the Orient to be sold in America or England and Spain. Portland thrived during this great era of sail. Maine timber provided masts for most of the sailing ships of the time and shipbuilding became a major industry down east. But the age of sail gave way at the turn of the century to the steam engine vessels developed during the Industrial Revolution. The beautiful, pristine wharfs of the eighteen hundreds gave way to the oil and coal of the new century and the shops and industrial buildings lining Commercial Street degraded to greasy bars and brothels. It became a red light district catering to the sailors of the world while Portland struggled with decay.

Today Portland is the financial and cultural capitol of the state and has risen from the ashes of an irrelevant waterfront ghetto during the first half of the twentieth century to a renovated, rejuvenated cultural center where industry and art flourish together. Commercial Street is clean and vibrant with nautical businesses, upscale shops and restaurants lining the wharfs while the Old Port section, with its old brick, wrought iron, narrow streets and quaint boutiques, remind us of its heritage. Artists and musicians display their crafts in the small parks amidst the granite gray office buildings of Congress Street and the financial district; a strange combination of Birkenstocks and dark blue suits. This is the city

Robert Erickson
Round Pond, ME

to which Jacqueline Gourdin brought her music and her life.

The night was a sultry but beautiful evening which was typical of Maine in August. We could smell the harbor but there was no sea breeze that night so it was a steaming harbor we sensed; hot, humid with nothing moving but the slow tide. We had parked our car a few blocks from the music studio and walked eagerly but slowly, having arrived early for the performance. Children were playing in the streets and on the sidewalks lined with young maples that arched over the walkway, giving the air the unusual combined fragrance of green growth and hot concrete.

My wife and I talked about Jacqui as we strolled; our beautiful Jacqui, recalling the events that had brought her to Portland just months before; events that might have emotionally crippled the faint of heart; events that would certainly have destroyed a music career and yes, maybe even a life. Portland was her goal, it always had been, even the many years before when she lived in Dorchester, a suburb of Boston, where we had first met her and where the emancipation of Jacqueline Gourdin had begun.

The studio was small and filled to capacity. The air conditioners labored to keep the hall cool but with limited success as several women used the concert programs as fans. Peoples' faces shined with the warmth but also with delight looking to the night's performance. As the lights dimmed the audience hushed in anticipation of an unusual recital featuring one piano, four hands. A gentleman stood on the stage and simply announced, "Ladies and gentlemen, Jacqueline Gourdin." And Jacqui took the stage to great applause. This petite lady in her sixties who couldn't have stood more than five feet one or two walked to her piano and placed a hand on the open side of the grand as though she were caressing something alive. She wore a simple light blue dress that complemented the blue wall color, her gray hair was pulled back in a bun which was part of her signature appearance and her mocha skin was aglow with pleasure and the night. There was a slight smile that exuded confidence and pleasure at once, a smile with which we were so familiar that said, "This is my domain, this is where I belong and you will see why." She didn't speak immediately, which was a practiced part of her stage presence that held the attention of everyone in the hall. First she made eye contact, looking at each row as though she personally knew each person there. She thanked all for coming in her soft, controlled stage voice that almost had a lilt of British; but no, more like the voice and diction of live theater. Then Jacqui, with a broad smile, introduced her four-hand partner for the evening, Keith Witherell. Keith walked briskly to Jacqui and bowed to the crowd. He was a big man who seemed an unlikely pianist who overemphasized Jacqui's petiteness but a person and partner in whom Jacqui had complete confidence and respect.

Keith was a product of Jacqui's tutelage starting his piano career with Jacqui at the age of seven and studying with her for eleven years before going on to his bachelors and masters degrees in music. Teacher and pupil were totally at ease as they sat at the bench and made several adjustments to accommodate the disparity in size; Keith to the treble side and Jacqui to the bass. The music was to begin.

The concert started with Variations by Beethoven which was received with thunderous applause, then a piece by Faure, Dolly Suite, then The Shubert Variations that was brilliant and the evening was to be complete with the Grande Sonata in F Minor, Opus 178 by Czerny. The Sonata began very melodious and the two pianists swayed to the rhythm almost as though they were somehow joined at the side. Jacqui turned the pages as necessary with the practiced hand of someone who had done so thousands of times; a flicking motion that never missed the page and was done so quickly that there was no interruption in her score. They were in true concert with each other as the tempo began to rise from adagio to the cut time finale. Their fingers seemed to fly over the keyboard in crescendo after crescendo as the

Robert Erickson
Round Pond, ME

swells of music grew more and more intense. Jacqui played with such force that the piano almost seemed to quiver under her fingers. I could feel the music reverberate in my chest as they gave their whole being to each musical swell. I watched our dear friend actually come off the bench as she struck one of the final chords. Her eyes were riveted to the score and the final notes were struck in perfect unison. Then it was over. The silence was an awesome contrast to that wonderful finale. In that silence there was a surprised pause. It was as if the audience was reeling from the emotion of the music from which they had to recover. And recover they did with tremendous applause, whistles and cries of "Bravo, Bravo." The two performers bowed and bowed to hands that would not stop their appreciation and despite their exhaustion played another short selection as a thank you for your enjoyment.

While they were playing I reflected on the life that brought Jacqui to this place, to this level of excellence; one which started in the ashes of black poverty and persistently struggled to self-actualization, success and fulfillment. Maybe that is why she loves Portland so much; they are very much alike.

Charles Boldreghini
Collierville, TN

Family Table

Fondly built by my own hand
To accommodate a family of twelve,
It saw many years of service
And bore silent witness
As beloved ones who around it sat
Matured and went their separate ways

Long since removed
From the place of honor
As the family hub
Where all gathered each day
For the evening meal,
It now stands alone, seldom used
Stored in an outbuilding.

But there are times
When, gazing at it, I glimpse,
Ten youthful faces,
And my attuned ear picks up sounds
Of a happy family dining.

Celine Rose Mariotti
Shelton, CT

The Long Aftermath

Fondly built
August was the month
It all went chaos
Katrina came and left
The Gulf Coast with a lot of triage
Left people without their homes
Cleaned them out financially,
Right to the bones

A state like Mississippi,
Struggling to leave
Their poverty behind
Poverty that kept them
Locked in time
Poverty that arrived
After the Civil War
So many in Mississippi
Are so poor,
Their delegation was on their feet
Fighting tooth and nail
They can't be beat!

New Orleans was trying
To dance and sing once again
Mardi Gras came back for a little while
Jazz and the blues are still in style
People long to one day return
To the City they love
That Ole' New Orleans
Is alive and well
They all have a story or two to tell

Celine Rose Mariotti
Shelton, CT

Poor Alabama left unheard from
The media big shots zoom in on New Orleans
But forget about Mobile and such
The Governor plows on
Trying to get money for his state
Oh, what will be Alabama's fate?

The Long Aftermath
Went on and on
Another month before the Hurricane season
Becomes renowned
Who will the Hurricanes tear apart?
Will the Government play it smart?
No one in Washington seems to care
Nothing about this was at all fair
Blame it on God
Who sends the storms
Blame it on the devil
He has horns
Blame it on the witch doctor
Who cast the spell
Blame it on the government
They are ne'er do well
Blame it on something
That might make sense
Blame it on the gods
It's ancient tense
But find a way to reach deep inside
Put another person at your side
Pray that disaster does not come
Pray that God's Will may be done

Celine Rose Mariotti
Shelton, CT

The Long Aftermath
May last a long time
The rebuilding of the Gulf Coast
Will cost many dimes
But this is our country
The Good Ole' USA
These are our citizens
Americans all
We need to work together
In a common goal
And put the Gulf Coast back together
As a whole.

***

Janice Babcock
Wauwatosa, WI

Perfect Plans

Poverty and abuse
Prevention needed

Partners' debate
Pursue discussion

People promote ideals
Present new ideas

Purposeful endeavors considered
Ponder their thoughts

Private goals prioritized
Partnership the answer

John Hagan
Springboro, OH

A Risk Well Taken

The mares turned their heads and necks indolently toward the approaching Jeep, as Gallagher advanced the four-wheel-drive vehicle through the fresh snow in the long lane and progressed steadily toward the antebellum farmhouse on this cold winter Saturday. Misty vapors emanated from the backs and nostrils of the horses while they yanked frozen timothy from the lean-to hayrack on the back of the barn. The chuck wagon was arriving, but until it produced some apple and alfalfa treats, Josie and Roxie had better fare to attend.

Gallagher eased into the barnyard, and departing the SUV, he made the first human footprints in the area when he stepped toward the hatch to allow Gypsy, his Border Collie, to bound from the cargo compartment. The hoarfrosted trees throughout the farm created a dazzling contrast with the cobalt sky, and the six inches of white powder that had fallen overnight shrouded the soybean stubs and formed undulating expanses of glistening snow diamonds on the rolling crop fields. The woodpile, bracketed by two walnut trees in the dooryard, was bedecked in snow with a baker's artistry, the white frosting cascading over and down the logs like vanilla icing might festoon the top and sides of a chocolate bundt cake. The snow on the farmhouse, summer kitchen, and horse barn gleamed in the sun, and the roofs seemed to cling to their soft blankets like the morning procrastinator cleaves to his quilts. The black paddock fence formed three drunken shadow lines in the unbroken snow, and a Red-Tailed Hawk shrieked while it surveyed the land in its relentless search for the unwary rodent that might poke its furry snout from the snow.

Michael Gallagher felt the bite of the fourteen-degree temperature almost immediately, but he would soon accustom to the outdoors after an hour's ride in his climate-controlled Jeep Patriot. He slipped on his knit hat and pulled up his sweatshirt hood before wiggling into a fleece-lined vest-coat that provided real warmth but allowed for unrestricted arm movement. Once bundled, Gallagher tromped over to the barn where he unlocked the tack room door and then threw open the two main doors to provide the horses access to their twelve-by-twelve-foot stalls. He climbed the haymow ladder and threw down a fresh bail of timothy to stuff into the stall racks. He then grabbed two halters and a lead rope from the tack room and walked to the lean-to stable door on the far left of the barn in order to bring the horses over to the alley-way. Now restrained by only the lift bar across the doorway of the stable, Roxie, the alpha horse, was waiting eagerly in front of Josie in anticipation of the apple-flavored biscuits and alfalfa cubes that she had heard Gallagher toss into the wall buckets. Knowing the drill perfectly, each horse offered her head willingly to the halter to expedite her access to fresh hay and bucket treats.

Gallagher actually resided about forty-five miles from the farm in a mid-sized city where he had been teaching high school English for over twenty-five years. The farm, which he had purchased purely as an investment about fifteen years before, had evolved into a labor of love, and Josie and Roxie, purchased seven and five years before respectively, were fulfilling a dream for Gallagher that dated to his early childhood. He hadn't ridden either of the horses since late fall when Jack Hendricks, his farrier, had pulled their shoes and trimmed their hooves for another winter. Once in their stalls, the nascent and ridiculous thought of riding one of the horses through the undisturbed snow around the bridle trail that wound through the ninety acres of crop fields, wood lots, and creek beds began to take hold in Gallagher's mind. His horseback riding was always an exercise in anxiety even in the company of a skilled rider on the most desirable days. The idea of a solo ride on a mid-January day was both preposterous and alluring, and even if he did try it, he wasn't sure which horse he would use. Josie, the twelve-year-old bay at 14.2 hands, was much less imposing to Gallagher, but Roxie, the frisky nine-year-old sorrel at well over 15 hands, was much better trained and a little less spooky.

The smooth snow carpet over the short grass of the bridle trail leading from the barnyard beckoned Gallagher like the sirens called to Odysseus, but Gallagher had no comrades, as the hero of *The Odyssey* had, to blunt the dangerous invitation. His only restraints were his inherent fears that for some kind of macho reason he was presently resolved to master. Even those who would urge him to suppress his anxieties would never suggest that he ride alone on a frozen, snow-covered surface. Having, however, seen a colorful photograph in a horse magazine of a beautiful cowgirl riding a sturdy steed through deep snow while leading a white pony, he now imagined himself on a similar ride. His reluctance in this and other daring matters had often reminded him of Rudyard Kipling's "Rikki-Tikki-Tavi," in which the muskrat Chuchundra cowers near the wall at night rather than traverse the room, fearing that the cobras Nag and Nagaina might be lurking nearby. Gallagher loathed his restricting aversion to risky adventures, and he chafed from his slavish attachment to humdrum security, which as Hecate says in *Macbeth* "is mortals' chiefest enemy."

"What the hell, I'm not gonna live forever," he said in false bravado to Gypsy, who lay in the scattered hay near the stalls with her black and white face resting between her forepaws. She seemed to know intuitively that Gallagher was planning something really stupid.

"Let's do it! Roxie, you're the lucky girl today."

Roxie turned her head from the hayrack in her stall and gave Gallagher a look that virtually said, "You've got to be kidding!"

Fetching a saddle, a blanket, and a bridle from the tack room, Gallagher returned to the alleyway and hooked Roxie

John Hagan
Springboro, Ohio

to the chain attached to one of the eight-by-eight-inch oak columns that intersected with the barn's crossbeams, using the old-fashioned fork-and-tongue, hole-and-peg connectors. As he brushed and saddled Roxie, Gallagher reflected upon the nature of the crucible before him. This was not a test he had to take; it wasn't a thesis defense before a graduate committee, nor a speech to parents at an open house, nor a forty-foot barn-roof climb for needed repairs. This challenge he could choose to ignore. It wasn't even the roller coaster ride at LeSourdsville Lake when he was six, the high-dive plunge at Miller's Grove Pool when he was eight, or the prom-date phone call to Megan O'Banion when he was seventeen. While those acts of extraordinary courage were entirely optional, they bore real merit and yielded delightful results (especially the call to Megan), but this was borderline lunacy.

He tightened the cinch a bit more and then swung a leg over Roxie and eased her out of the barn and into the barnyard. Gypsy darted before them, crisscrossing, pirouetting, and yapping in her typically irrepressible enthusiasm. Roxie ignored her for the most part, but the mare would not be averse to taking a shot with a hind hoof at the rambunctious canine if the opportunity arose. Gallagher carefully zigzagged Roxie down the hill from the barnyard, avoiding a direct descent that might cause slippage. He had literally been holding his breath until they entered the bridle path proper and began the second hill that would take them down to the straightaway that led them along the creek meandering through the wood line on their right. Once on the straightaway, Gallagher began singing the theme song from *Sugarfoot*, one of the television westerns he watched as a kid. He had it on good authority that singing to his horses while trail riding sometimes eased their fears and disguised his own, and most of the time it seemed to work. His repertoire of theme songs also included those from *Cheyenne* and *Bronco Lane.*

As they proceeded along the trail, Roxie occasionally

turned her head toward Gallagher, seeming to ask if he really wanted to take this ride, but she showed no signs of fractiousness, and she moved ahead with minimal urging. Gallagher's mindset was somewhere between guarded confidence and devout prayer. At length, he began to absorb the surroundings he hoped to enjoy in his private adventure. The land was truly inspiring; everything seemed to glisten in the sun, and the hush that fell over the farm from the fluffy snow and breezeless air suggested a Currier and Ives landscape. He watched a crimson Cardinal light upon a low hanging tree branch that extended over the bridle trail about thirty yards before him. He knew Roxie saw it too, and the bird played Chicken with the horse until it tired of the game and took flight to another perch that Gallagher couldn't see but the Red-Tailed Hawk probably could. In some ways he wished he were sharing it all with someone, but he knew that would defeat his purpose.

At the end of the straightaway, he angled Roxie to the left around a bend and headed back up the farm lane before bearing right into another bean field and onto the bridle trail again. Gypsy continued to dart back and forth and create little snow squalls in her wake, offering an occasional yap or two at nothing in particular. As he started up the gentle grade on the far side of the bean field, Gallagher heard the first and then the second reports from a muzzleloader somewhere beyond the woods to his right, probably on the Ruble property. He had forgotten that Saturday through Tuesday were the four muzzleloader days of a deer-hunting season that would return to a bow-only restriction on Wednesday. He'd no sooner said, "Keep your eyes peeled for deer" to Gypsy, Roxie, and himself than an eight-point buck bounded from the woods about twenty yards in front of him on his right and then across the bridle path into the beans. Gypsy barked, and he panicked, but Roxie only slowed and held her course.

"Good girl, Roxie!" he said to the mare as he stroked her

neck.

What happened next came from the blue. Roxie had just started forward at a faster pace when she bolted to the left and into the bean field. As she did, Gallagher stayed on for a few yards before he went backwards off the rump of his horse. The ground came up fast and hard, and the rider went down on his shoulder and neck. The pain was instant and blinding, and for about ten seconds, he could feel nothing below his neck and shoulder. *I've got to get up,* he thought wildly, *or I may be paralyzed.* As he did, he ran about ten yards to test his mobility, all the while shaking his right arm to regain some feeling. He became only gradually conscious of Gypsy's hysterical barking and Roxie's frantic whinnying. When he recovered somewhat, he saw Gypsy in a defensive stance and Roxie now snorting and stomping, her reins hanging loosely and dragging. Gallagher then saw the reason for the buck's desperate flight. Five coyotes had quickly formed a rough cordon around the horse, rider, and dog. They had obviously been in pursuit of the buck when in the throes of their hunger they had found easier prey.

"Oh, hell! Now what!"

With military precision, the coyotes began their concentric circling around Gallagher, Gypsy, and Roxie. Gypsy continued her barking while she darted toward and retreated from the coyotes, taking up the defense of man, horse, and herself. Roxie continued to stomp her front hooves, her reins now whipping like fly fishing lines off the sides of her thrashing head. For his part, Gallagher had nothing for self-defense, and his neck and arm were now throbbing from the stinger sustained from the fall. He threw snow at the coyotes, but it was far too powdery to have any effect. As they eased forward, the predators began their low growls and bared their sharp incisors and long canines. Suddenly, two went for Gypsy, and she became a blur in a two-on-one fight that escalated so fast that Gallagher couldn't react to the mismatch. His head turned involuntarily toward Roxie when she roared, and he watched an airborne coyote the mare had launched perfectly with a hind leg and hoof. When the furry projectile landed about twenty feet away, it whined pitifully and joined a pack mate in a gimpy and tail-between-legs retreat to the woods. As Gallagher turned again toward Gypsy, he saw the fifth coyote advancing toward the out-numbered dog. Gallagher sprang at the coyote and kicked its side, sending it wailing and running across the bean field. With adrenaline pumping, he moved quickly toward Gypsy and threw himself onto one of the coyotes, which squirted from his grasp, and the dog's remaining combatant led the coyote twosome in a judicious departure.

Gallagher rolled over on his back in the snow and stared up into the blue sky. He was soon looking into the soft brown eyes of his loving companion, which, with the exception of a few face and ear scratches, seemed none-the-less for the tussle.

"Damn, I love you, Gypsy!"

Gallagher pulled the dog down onto his chest, and she shoved her snout into his neck and shoulder like she did so often on the floor at home. Within a minute he heard the familiar nicker of his other friend who had done herself proud as well. He rose to his feet and walked to Roxie. Gathering her reins, Gallagher said to the sorrel mare, "Remind me not to rile you, Rox. You're one nasty lady when you get your back up."

He wrapped his arms around her neck and buried his face in her withers. She seemed to know how pleased he was with her.

"I love you too, babe!"

Gallagher swung himself into the saddle and headed back to the bridle path where it soon wound into the woods and out again to where it bordered a fifteen-acre timothy field. After coyote combat, just trail riding, even in snow, seemed like a walk in the park. As he rode, he watched Gypsy before him. Lissome as a willow, she had taken the lead again while keeping him in sight. Her nose to the ground, she was already searching for fun as her jaunty rag tail bounced in rhythm with her gait. Roxie appeared to have formed a discernable respect for her fearless defender who had always yapped and nipped at her from the other side of the paddock fence. Gallagher surmised that a bond had been established among the horse, dog, and man.

Before reaching the horse barn, Gallagher began to reflect on his decision to ride on such a day. Easing Roxie up to the tie post, he looked at Josie in her stall and said, "Well, my dear, you missed quite a ride today." She looked up only briefly before shoving her nose back into the hayrack. Gallagher now began to feel the intense cold again for the first time since before the ride, and he slipped the bridle, saddle, and blanket quickly from Roxie. He handed her a few cubes of alfalfa from a Gatorade cooler on a bench as he brushed her down and then turned her and Josie out behind the barn.

When he walked back into the alleyway, he said to the resting Gypsy, "Well, sweetie, I finally ran into the middle of the room today, and I think old Kipling would be proud of me, but I'd have to tell that muskrat he's right. Nag and Nagaina are out there, and sometimes the snakes beat you and sometimes you beat the snakes. I just don't think I'll test my luck again for awhile."

After re-stuffing the hayrack on the back of the barn, Gallagher took Gypsy up to the house and swabbed her scratches with peroxide. She accepted his attentions gratefully and patiently. He then closed up the house and put Gypsy in the backseat of the Jeep. As he started down the long lane for home, he began thinking about that early-April night many years before when he had mustered the courage to call Megan O'Banion to ask her to the senior prom. His gumption today yielded some of the fruits that telephone call provided. The gratification he felt as he returned to the horse barn with his steadfast pals was much like the satisfaction

John Hagan
Springboro, OH

he gained from walking into Wampler's Dance Barn with a prom date his government teacher would tell him the following Monday was "the most beautiful girl at the dance."

Turning from the lane onto the county road, he recalled the smiling image of an ageless girl and thought, *Thank you Megan, for not dashing my hopes or crushing my spirit as a teenager! Your response to my phone call provides lingering memories of a risk well taken, and it just inspired another. It's a funny thing about pretty girls; you have no way of knowing how your charms will one day be the delight of an aging man's reverie.*

Glancing over his shoulder at the backseat, Gallagher could see that Gypsy had already hunkered down into the blankets that he kept there to protect the upholstery and comfort his pooch. Where else but in the companionship of a faithful dog would he find such unqualified devotion?

"Love ya, Gyps!"

The tail swished a bit, and the ears perked a little, but the eyes remained closed.

***

Lou Roach
Poynette, WI

Affirmation

Spring's golden moon
climbs winter-bare branches,
brightens the night with lambent light
and subtle colors not seen since autumn.
The soft glow hints of another April
when I dared answer "Yes."

Mary Lyons
Biddeford, ME

Sailing the Land

I am sailing the land
Floating down the Kennebec Valley
Through the soft, soft greens of spring.

I am being pulled from the Thruway
Streaming up to Canada
In the vivid hills of New York autumn.

I am melting off the road
Coasting up and down the Berkshires
In the unrelenting blue of summer sky.

I am dreaming off Route One
Leaning to the Bay
In the cold clear gray of winter.

I am drifting off the path
Seeing fawns and eating raspberries
In the wishing you back of every season.

Mary Jo Balistreri
Waukesha, WI

Sunset Over the Mill Pond

On the dock, a woman watches feathers of snow geese
stream across a fire-darkening sky,
red torch of sun about to burn out.
A few last flames halo treetops along the shore
and the pond becomes
a prism of muted yellows,
oranges, alizarin crimson. Swallowing silence,
a woman's breath
slows like the banked embers along the horizon.

Night blinds her until everything is sound.
A whippoorwill's repetitive call,
carp slapping against pond's edge,
a loon's cry for his mate that echoes across the water,
all tangled within the brushed voices
of memory, tucked beneath the wash of time...
She thinks of them,

her grandsons, their lives and deaths. Fireflies fall
from the trees, light up and go out, light up and go
out.
So short these signals of love.

Lisa Vihos
Sheboygan, WI

A Brief History of Mail

Once upon a time, there were
smoke signals and bird calls
and charred bones left on mossy

cairns. These early equivalents of
"alert the media" did their best
to convey the ebb and flow

of human endeavor in those grand,
nomadic days before the invention
of tampons and sliced bread.

Gradually, we realized we needed
to move our words a bit faster
and so we got the ponies involved.

These express equines dragged
our words toward the industrial age,
though they still needed to be shod

and curry-combed and fed an apple
now and then. We got the philatelists
on the case and soon, stamp collecting

was born. For a long time, we cruised
along, with rates rising a penny a year
and the occasional someone going postal.

Insanity aside, our mail options
have now advanced to texting
and sexting and tiny tweets.

Lisa Vihos
Sheboygan, WI

And so we have returned to the birds.
Sender and receiver beware: burnt bones
crossed on fire pits may not be far behind.

***

Kristina Selting
Richfield, MN

Don't Wait

If now be the hour of our discontent, what
drags our weighted steps and gives us pause?
To part our feelings from our sleeves and
in the moment shine—How many times do
moments slip away...when our tongue is held
by fear or time...the things we think and do not say.
Who among us have spoken blindly with
No regret...in anger or in jest. Perchance.
Is it civility then, or pride that grips our heart
and fills our soul with the pangs of past regret.
As the hour draws near...our mortality begs us,
"Pray you—find the courage deep inside—to give
you the strength to share with the ones that need to hear."
The hour is relentless, and no one is exempt...
Work now to make the moments count so
you may rest in peace...

Jeanine Stevens
Sacramento, CA

Key West

We ignore raccoons ripping
food lockers in camp,
lay in this ocean, a warm, salt cushion,
like a bread bath, moist,
even wet enough
to make yeast rise and fish flower.
Chartreuse air pockets
welcome our bodies we navigate
next to sharpest coral.
Distant thoughts of the north woods
return. We float in memory
on Lake Winnebogosh,
avoid black leeches, and acrid skunks
sniffing under our wood cabin.
That day gone, this one remains,
a flushed solid eternity: red mangroves,
roseate spoonbill sky,
white ibis and a solitary blue heron.
Convolutions in sand
immense as mountains, caress
our toes, rocking ripples
forever holding this shore.

Fritz Burke
Appleton, ME

A Eulogy for Richard Gould

At Richard Gould's funeral the cars and pickups were lined up for half a mile on both sides of the Searsmont Road. I had to park down in the village and jog back up to the church, feeling like a heel because I was late and also because I was carrying a notebook, which laid bare my intention of taking advantage of Richard (who had done me so many favors over the years) one last time. Writing can be a dirty trade. I felt like a vulture.

I knew Richard mostly through my other trade in the construction business. Richard was a ground guy, and on the occasions when we worked the same job site, I would arrive in the morning to find Richard perched on some backhoe or bulldozer, already hard at work.

Richard had to work long days because he spent so much time talking. He was a good storyteller—probably because he got so much practice—and since he was a man of strong opinions and not shy about stating them, his stories were often about the screw-ups of other construction workers, or town officials, or anyone else that Richard found lacking in common sense.

"Aaaagh," Richard would say. And then after a dramatic pause, "I seen it right off." Aaaagh was Richard's signature utterance, but I'm afraid it's impossible to translate. It was a sound, both triumphant and fatalistic, that began in the back of the throat and rolled off the roof of the mouth. Into its long gargly vowel Richard managed to express nearly everything that is tragic and foolish in the human condition.

Richard said Aaaagh to me the last time I talked with him, right after it came out in conversation that I had spent much of the last month lying on a beach in Mexico. Richard did not approve of lying around on beaches. I doubt Richard ever even stood around on a beach—unless he was putting in a septic system at some summer home on one of the lakes. Just the image of Richard Gould in a bathing suit is like imagining a nun sporting a push-up bra. Comical. But in a sacrilegious way.

Richard did approve of hard work, of taking care of family, of being a good neighbor and citizen, and although not a churchgoer was, never-the-less, a man guided by his own honorable and compassionate code. This is essentially what Pastor Adolphson of the Appleton Baptist Church was saying as he gave Richard's eulogy. He spoke of how Richard donated the land adjacent to his house for the church's driveway and parking area, and of Richard's many other good deeds, none of which surprised me.

The list of Richard's good deeds was long, and as the pastor spoke I looked around the church. I knew most of the people, but it was odd to see them all dressed up. There were women with muscular forearms sticking out of the short sleeves of summer dresses, and men squirming uncomfortably in suit jackets that didn't fit right and whose bad haircuts I had never noticed before since I had never seen them uncapped. I had a view of Richard as well in the open casket. His eyeglasses where perched on his hooked nose so that he seemed to be peering out one last time past his children and grandchildren and great-grandchildren. Out through the open door at the back of the church and across the meadowy fringe of his pasture where, in testimony to his years of hard work, his collection of retired snow plows, dump trucks, and tractors lay moldering in the high July grass.

It was strange to be in Richard's presence for so long and not hear him talk. And it saddened me to think that in these politically correct times, when so much of the color of our words has been washed out, that I would never hear Richard's straight talk again. If Richard thought somebody a fool he said so. But he didn't rush to judgment. He knew that surfaces could be misleading and that you had to dig down

Fritz Burke
Appleton, ME

to the root of things to discover the truth. Sometimes the digging could be done with a backhoe. And sometimes it took years of plowing roads, of town meetings and bean suppers and reading between the lines of small-town gossip—for a more considered opinion to emerge.

After Richard was loaded into the hearse we headed over to the cemetery. A few people spoke—the quick story that sums up something essential about the deceased. I didn't want to intrude on the private affair of family and close friends so I held my tongue. But I'm going to work my story in here.

I met Richard when I first moved to Appleton and was camped out building my family's home. I was on a tight budget and pressed for time, since my wife's pregnancy was progressing faster than the house. It was a hot day in a hot summer and I was back filling, with a wheelbarrow and shovel, a small concrete-block foundation. I was also wishing for a backhoe.

Sure enough, a backhoe came rumbling along the road and stopped in front of my driveway. It was Richard, who was Road Commissioner at the time, peering suspiciously over his machinery at what looked to me like just another bump in the road. Richard didn't like the look of it though, and he set in digging until he had unearthed a boulder the size of a wood cook-stove. He prized and pushed and rolled it around until he finally managed to nudge it to the side of the road. Then he idled the diesel down and turned to where I stood watching and waiting for the chance to ask him about working a back fill job in when he was done digging up the road.

"Aaaagh," he said. "I seen it right off."

I guess a year or so went by before I paid Richard back for back filling my foundation. Typically, he never quoted me a price and didn't seem worried about collecting. Whenever I mentioned it to him, he put me off. Eventually, I stopped down to his house, determined to settle up.

Richard was sitting by the woodstove, and we talked—or

Fritz Burke
Appleton, ME

rather Richard talked and I listened. Finally, when he stopped to take a breath, I seized the moment and asked him about my bill.

But instead he told me about an elderly woman with a barn roof that was leaking on her goats.

"She doesn't have much money," he said, giving me a long look.

Well, I seen it right off. But it took Richard to point it out.

And I saw also, on that warm summer afternoon last week as Richard was lowered into the earth, that a life spent working hard and of having the courage to speak about and the generosity to act upon the things he saw was Richard's legacy. A gift, rippling out from the circle of family and friends and neighbors and citizens until all of us, whether we knew Richard or not, are the beneficiaries.

***

Dianisha Leonard
Worcester, MA

Letting Go

Like a baby bird nestled close to his mother's breast,
I have to care and comfort you.
Though it may hurt me in the end,
I have to let you fly.
Unhappiness will consume you if given the chance,
I will not let this happen.
Tears swell behind eyes filled with so much pain,
my heart desires to give you peace.

Susann Pelletier
Lewiston, ME

Hurricane Weather

The hurricane has not hit yet—
I ask when?
Knowing how this closeness with you
Of word and breath
Presages
A mighty wind, great fluttering of leaves,
Falling of limbs,
And of the walls of all those rooms
That enclose our sleep,
Hold in our dreams.

I mean, all these extravagancies of summer
Becoming keener, will be upended
Petal by petal, whistle by whistle, call by call.
Roses and bobolinks and crickets
All hauled into the spiraling.
Daughters and sons, fathers and mothers,
More distant relations, neighbors and bosses
Drawn up
Into a final fandango
Before they go into the gust.

But I will go straight to the hurricane's eye,
Flying through the fiercest turning,
Arrive at the clear silence in the middle
And waltz there with you
Where only sky will clothe us
Where no words, no poems,
Will fall from our tongues...
Only the hum of old songs
We thought we had forgotten,
Only the sough of summer wind
On our lips.

Emily B. Ellis
Lewiston, ME

Maggie's Dream

I waited faithfully for your return
didn't touch your bowl
your bone
my head upon the couch sank low
let time pass
as I watched them pace
heard them mumbling your name
they didn't know
how I listened, how I prayed
then finally I heard the engine
saw them plodding up the stairs
just two
I knew that you would not be back
and I would be alone.

wandered over to my blanket
sniffing as I circled
round, round and round
lay down, felt a different kind of tired
a different weight upon my shoulders
she knelt, hand gentle on my head
stroking, soothing, rubbing
but it didn't stop the pain

how do I heal this wound
this hole that deepens, widens
every step on walks we knew by heart
my heart, so brimming
with the gloried scents we shared
noses buried inside snow
tufts of grass

(continued)

Emily B. Ellis
Lewiston, ME

hills of leaves
now so scattered,
no retrieving

they say I see in black and white
or maybe only gray
though in my dreams of you
the colors run, jump, leap
so fast
so strong
so bright
this is how I am remembering
how you live within me
rest beside me—
race you to the moon.

***

sarah p. roy
Oakland, ME

Tiger

Darkness overtakes
the shadow of dreams.
i am where i must be,
embracing passion—
shunning reality.

You ask,
Where is the Tiger?

He stirs in me.

Earl Weigelt
Winslow, ME

Honest Like Sawdust

And those fine little chips just flew
and piled-up under the saw
forming drift after drift
as each snarling storm
chewed the great logs into lengths.

Bone white and orange
and pleasant to touch;
to fill the hands with and squeeze
as the aroma arises and reaches the nose,
the finer dust riding the breeze.

Saw gas and oil
all sponged by the stuff,
and sweat and tree blood and wool—
"chore smells" they are, and nostalgic too,
a physic somehow to the soul.

Yellow birch mingles
with ash and rock maple,
some beech and black cherry thrown in...
a fine mound of stovewood grown higher and higher,
bound for the shed once it's split.

And when in midwinter in subarctic gloom
the frigid dark outstrips the daylight
and the lake grumbles outside and branches explode
and hoarfrost makes art on your windows,
another stick in the stove will stave off the cold
and you'll smile as you put on the coffee!

Hilary Carr
Rockport, ME

Sage

We had spent the past week attending doctor's appointments searching for a way to palliate his pain. It was bad now, constant and foreboding. The choices were stark. It was either an amputation or mounting, excruciating pain. The doctors warned that with his precarious heart condition he would probably not live through an amputation. But how could he sustain the living torture he was now enduring? Either way, his future hung in the balance and its heaviness permeated all our thoughts.

The care of his feet was paramount. These same feet that had taken my inquisitive dad around the world and back were now dark and gangrenous, lifeless. His world was now confined to an armchair. I helped Mother perform the daily rituals; bringing in the basin of warm water, washing and patting his feet dry, easing the soft fingers of lamb's wool carefully between his old toes, wrapping them in a loose white sock, sliding on the old slippers, now slit to encase his feet lightly.

My visit was ending. I packed my things and got ready to leave, dressed up for the trip, as was the custom in those days. Then I went in to spend the last hour or so sitting with Dad. It surprised me when he asked me to go drive him to Point Lobos, just the two of us.

"Do we have time?" I was worried about missing my flight.

"Of course," he insisted.

"Should I change?" I asked.

"Don't bother," he said. "Let's go!"

He loved Point Lobos. It was his sanctuary. Determination got him through the difficult logistics from chair to wheelchair to car. It put him into a sweat. We set out in his old yellow Buick, sharing the long front seat, looking ahead.

Hilary Carr
Rockport, ME

With a sideways glance I could see the deep green tourmaline of his wedding ring pulsing on the seat between us, long slim fingers clinching in pain, opening and closing. We blinked back tears. It reminded me of my ten year old moment with him at the Met when his beloved Renata Tebaldi sang his favorite aria from La Traviata. He had nudged me to pay particular attention. I remember watching my quiet engineer of a father crying openly in sheer delight.

We drove on in silence. Words jammed in my throat, wooden and dry. When at last we reached the Allen Memorial Grove he signaled me to stop.

"You walk the path," he said. "I'll wait here."

And that was how it went.

I set out running down the path, awkward and wobbly in my high heels, my suit, the costumes of my city life. Now I was sobbing, his clear instructions ringing in my ears.

"Don't miss the sage before the path opens wide into the glen.

"At the opening you will see the old Cyprus looking witchier than ever, bent over and knarled, propped up with wires now. Stop there. This marks the spot where you can see and hear the sea lions barking across from Seal Rock. They are magnificent."

I took a breath here and watched as the enormous animals sunned and squawked, hanging off their rocky ledge. Then I checked my watch and hurrying I set out again. His words came back.

"As you head out to the point be careful...the dirt path is steep and narrow.

Let the wind fill your ears. Sit down out there and notice the tiny tough ice plant and see how it manages to cling to the rocks and thrive. It should be in full bloom now."

He's right, I thought. *He knows this path so well. He loves mesembryanthemum. It is partly for its color and its tenacious grip on life, against all odds, so like him now, and partly because it took us all so long to learn its name and that had*

Hilary Carr
Rockport, ME

pleased him tremendously.

"This is the best place to view big Pacific rollers as they build in from the west.

"You'll taste the salty spume on your lips."

His voice urged me on.

"Around the corner is the deep crevasse the ocean has etched out. It has made the perfect place for the otters to dive and play in the waves. Some of them manage to surge in and out on the surf while they crack their abalone shells and scoop out a meal."

I stopped again. Otter families frolicked below, carelessly and easily. My insides were out of sync with this tempo of life. I resisted looking at my watch, but knots in my stomach warned me of the time slipping away. Why couldn't I just be here?

I headed over the stone path through the Cyprus grove and heard his words again:

"Go slowly through this primeval place. Check the moss and lichen of undisturbed years.

"It will open to another cove that is much quieter, more protected. There is a great spot to sit and watch the gulls screech as they scavenge for their perfect dinner. Then the path will lead you back through low lying bracken. Notice the whiff of sage everywhere.

"This is where I snip the cuttings that I stuff in my letters to you. I'll be waiting here. Take your time."

Flying away that afternoon I walked his path a thousand times. I had felt so torn running through Dad's sanctuary without him by my side, knowing that this had been the final hour, the last good-bye. I had so wanted words, a blessing, and a heart to heart exchange. As I write this reflection now, thirty two years later, I can still close my eyes, smell the sage, hear the bark of the sea lions, taste the salt of the giant Pacific rollers, and hear my dad's voice, a gift beyond words.

Jean Lawrence
Waldoboro, ME

Broad Bay Beginnings

No town, no church, no accommodations awaited them
as the *Lydia* sailed up Broad Bay in 1742.
Only wilderness, a touch of autumn color, a few inhabited cabins,
and small clearings were found
as they came seeking land, home, and hearth, a place to call their own.

***

Late October light showed an unending wilderness of ever greens
when the ship neared the Schenck's Point anchor age.
What appeared before the eyes of those few German migrants
did not meet expectations.
A sense of betrayal must have inched into their thoughts and hearts.
Promised long houses for winter shelter, a "city" with a church
were nowhere to be seen.
Only stones, stumps, and untenanted wilderness stood watch
as they came seeking land, home, and hearth, a place to call their own.

***

Jean Lawrence
Waldoboro, ME

Mother Nature gave a respite of eight weeks for the erection
of crude cabins:
floors of clay or flat stone with rough timber walls
chinked with straw and mud.
The land from the Point up the east side of the river
was parceled out in broad farm tracts.
Activity began, winter came, and the river froze.
Ice blocked all communication with the outside world.
The settlers struggled to survive
while seeking land, home, and hearth, a place to call
their own.

***

Indian raids, politics, disease, and the never-ending stones
did not overwhelm these pioneers.
Simple mills at the falls were built for sawing needed
timber,
gardens were planted, and cattle tended
as life flickered along the river's shores.
These hardy souls persevered;
they had come for land, home, and hearth, a place to
call their own.

***

Years passed and the *Priscilla* and *St. Andrews* brought
fifty more eager souls to settle on the Dutch Man's
Neck.
The river was charted, land surveyed, and hearths were
laid.
Their numbers and hopes swelled,
and at the head of the tide, a town was born.
The migrants had found a place of their own, a home.

Judith Canty Graves
Wayland, MA

The Yearning

There are times when
my soul yearns for
something that is almost
inexpressible, intangible, and fleeting.
I have a yearning
for past places and times,
especially from my childhood and youth.
Is this a symptom
of late middle age,
before the senior years begin?
I yearn for my hometown of childhood,
of places I used to know:
the secret beach, the cove on the bay,
my house in the woods.
These are indelible memories,
never to be forgotten.
I sense these places as if I were there now.
They are that real to me.
The paradox is,
they have slipped away
as the clouds slip away in the sky.
Everything that felt so
permanent, so real, so lasting
is gone now
and has been gone for years.
Why do I yearn for these places?
They are a connection to my being,
to my earliest years,
to my identity.
I felt secure and loved.
I felt my place in the world was right.

(continued)

Judith Canty Graves
Wayland, MA

My family was together.
During this time
I used to fall asleep listening
to the spring peepers as a child.
It was a time of innocence
that I cherish,
knowing now how impermanent the world is.
I accept the changes that have come with loss.
I age and lose people and places.
But the losses make
my life more real and precious.
As I yearn for the places of my past,
I also yearn to live
my present life to the fullest.

***

Gerry Rita Di Gesu
West Chatham, MA

Fear of Flying

Over capricious sheets of foam
flight I ache to share
feet planted on a sturdy board
the windsurfer's lone translucent wing
grabs the wind—
soars flies leap-frogs
across roiling steel-gray seas
racing clouds to the horizon

Karen Lewis Foley
Topsham, ME

Losing Hearing

The world becomes a mostly silent movie.
Breezes and hieroglyphs,
the smell of thyme underfoot
and a bird seeming to sing.
The trees move their leaves
turning green and silver silent sides.

Walkers in the distance with moving
mouths. One waves. You figure out
by where the hand or eye is aimed
whether or not to wave back.

Company dissolves, a sounding soup.
Unfenced vowels, partially
possible consonants.
Stretching and testing, you fall in.
Lost at sea, you dog paddle in clashing currents.
Little waves slap you silly
one by one by one.

Belva Ann Prycel
Alna, ME

The Claw

I suppose I should have left it there, the claw. I suppose I should have never picked it off the bottom of the tidepool, turned it over, or scraped my fingers along the chitinous serrated pincer. I should certainly never have taken it back to my porch and let it dry in the sun in a spot where I passed it on my way to the garden. It really didn't belong.

First, it was too big, larger than the lobster claws one normally finds at the pounds across the harbor, more massive than the usual tourist fare one got served at the lobster dock. In fact, as claws go, it was gigantic, and although it was cooked, it was not shattered, never cracked by a butter-slathered diner, never deconstructed in the usual way such appendages are eaten.

So it was something of an anomaly, and I unwisely took it home. That was my first mistake.

On the back porch it dried for a good part of the summer, although if it shrunk at all it was in the most undetectable way. The dogs expressed an interest in it for awhile, pausing in their mad rush out the kitchen door as if some olfactory brake had been applied, then relieving themselves and sniffing mightily over the claw remains. But soon, even they became indifferent.

For me, however, it was an uncomfortable reminder, an artifact which activated all the neurons of my aging brain, firing memories of so many disturbing fiddler crab encounters of years past on the Delaware Bay, times when thousands of fiddlers would traverse the marshes in a black wave after a heavy rain, or tie up traffic as they bisected the highway to scale the hills of neighboring farm fields. Always they were waving their huge right claws, and always in a curiously malevolent mood.

The claw has an attitude of open protest that reminds me

Belva Ann Prycel
Alna, ME

of all that, fully splayed, likely the last act of an angry lobster before sinking in the roiling stew of the lobster pot, a final gesture of defiance and rage. And why not? For this is surely a horrid way for any creature to die, even one as unsympathetic and morphologically different from us as a lobster. I considered this as I looked across the harbor at the scores of happy tourists, blithely eating away on these strange crustaceans, laughing and amicably enjoying a Maine summer day.

And then I remembered the second mistake, and the unplanned visit to Pemaquid Point on that innocuous August day when we first moved here—the experience that still inspires more than one bad dream and questioning moment. It wasn't expected of course, and it wasn't really wanted, the experience there, but it reminded me that my comfortable little world, and my measurement of it, are severely constricted by a narrow understanding of time. I had been there to Pemaquid, a few times before, watching sunsets and sketching waves, sitting on the rocks with the gulls who always seemed to be facing seaward with me. But on this day, a visit of friends "from away," necessitated that I do more than my usual rock sitting or wave watching. They were sightseers, here to "experience Maine" they said, which I took in their vernacular to mean a lobster for every meal and a visit to all the prime tourist destinations. The latter included not only seeing the lighthouse at Pemaquid, but tediously mulling over all the maritime artifacts in the museum at its base. I confess I had never done this myself, having already seen enough antique lobster traps, tackle blocks, and old photos of Pemaquid to satisfy my curiosity for years. But being a good hostess, I reluctantly went along.

That was the crux of the second mistake. It was, truth be told, not a bad decision at first, for I learned more about lobstering from the cheerful woman who manned the museum than I had expected to encounter. She stood, this petite, gray-haired gentle lady, among the fish spears, giant hooks and grisly entrapments of a bygone fishing industry, with photos of iced in schooners and gutted Atlantic cod, dismasted wrecks and tangled rigging, and recited in the most genteel way the history of lobstering on the coast of Maine. It was a long recitation, but not as long as the time lobstering had been going on here. And in these cold northern waters, depleted of virtually everything else that is edible, these feisty crustaceans were now the dominant species. Survivors.

I considered this as I looked out the lighthouse window at lobster boats coming and going amid miles of buoys, some so dangerously dense on the waters that it was hard to imagine how any boat could navigate here. Yet somehow, as every other fishery had suffered depletion and collapse, the lobster business had been able to continue.

Perhaps this is because lobsters are scavengers and able to eat almost anything disgusting that falls to the bottom, as well as tolerating the extreme conditions of northern winters. They obviously have such a tough carapace that they are unattractive to all but the hardiest of predators, and are only most vulnerable when molting. This leaves them, as lowly bottom dwellers, now virtually the only item on the food chain. But it was not always so.

In the not very distant past, when other marine life abounded in the north, the lobster was considered a kind of primitive junk food. Native Americans ate them, but generally preferred other fare when they could get it. And in the 1800's, prisoners in the penal system were known to stage revolts over being served too much lobster as a regular food item. Only in the 20th century did the lobster achieve a certain discreet desirability, appearing on restaurant menus and diverse eating venues, and even then it was amazingly cheap to come by. As recently as 30 years ago in Maine, a dollar could get you a lobster dinner with all the accoutrements. Now, however, that is not the case.

While I'm considering the expense of taking our friends to another lobster feast, our amiable tour guide is continuing

Belva Ann Prycel
Alna, ME

her dissertation on lobsters, informing us that the catch will probably be good this year, as new regulations permit only the taking of juvenile lobsters, allowing the youngest to mature and the oldest to remain and reproduce. And it is at about this juncture in her story that I have the unfortunate occasion to look away from the window and toward a corner of the room. It is here, cast in partial shadow, that a yellowed photograph of indeterminate age hangs in sepia drabness. It is of a young girl, seven or eight years old, and she is standing before a weathered shed, smiling shyly at the camera. Beside her, nailed to the shed wall, are two objects that stagger the consciousness, the carapaces of two gargantuan lobsters, arms extended on either side, reaching from the ground to over the top of the girls head.

As if to fully intimidate the viewer and forever seal the fear, beneath the photo in a glass case rests a giant claw, over a foot in width and at least two feet long. I will never look at a lobster in quite the same way again.

On idle nights, I sometimes wonder if the tiny land-adapted fiddler crab had achieved the physical stature of the lobster, would those testy throngs have passed me so harmlessly on the marsh roads of long ago? Or if the northern lobsters had banned into socialized armies like the fiddlers, would they so tragically be duped into the confines of the lobster pot? Either way, some things may have worked to our advantage as a predator species on the food chain, and against the crab.

Yet when I think of the claw at Pemaquid Point, and remember the angry fiddlers, I wonder...

I place the claw on the back porch in a bucket with some shells and stones for camouflage and vow to quickly return it to the harbor.

Some debris, along with some thoughts, may best be left at the edge of the tidepool.

Genie Dailey
Jefferson, ME

Contemplating Stones

I wonder why poets don't write about stones.
To me, they're intriguing; they speak to me
In colors and textures unique and appealing.
Rosy and rusty, burnished and crusty; white, black, and marbled—
I have to pick them up.
I have to hold them in my hands and hear what they can tell me.

From the heart and the heat of Earth's creation,
They've pushed their way up and into our awareness.
Now they live alongside us, enjoying and enduring
The same things we encounter—
The happy babble of brooks and babies;
Warmth from the sun and from family and friends;
Stormy days and fickle, flighty winds;
Omnipotent oceans and towering hills.

We wander among them, these primeval, variegated stones,
Seeking their messages, yearning to understand.
We pick them up, hold them and turn them over in our hands;
We take in their coolness or their heat,
Their smoothness, wetness, grittiness, crevices, veins.

In their subtle silence, stones speak to us.

Genie Dailey
Jefferson, ME

Watch Their Eyes

Written after visiting
the Holocaust and Human Rights Center of Maine,
June 2010

Flickering film clips haunt me still,
black-and-white images of ordinary people
going about the business of their lives
in an era I can barely comprehend—it was
before I was born.

Well-dressed men and women bustle about the city,
all appearing normal except for one thing:
each bears a yellow star upon their breast—
no hope of blending into the crowds,
of escaping notice by soldiers and police.
"Juden," says the star.
Watch their eyes.

When things get worse, the lucky ones
are herded into boxcars for a journey
some will not survive for lack of air and
abundance of filth.
But the promise of life in a labor camp
is better than death on their own doorsteps.
Although confused and fearful,
they hope to return to their homes
after the war.
Watch their eyes.

Genie Dailey
Jefferson, ME

In the end, those who still live are freed,
leaving behind the ashes and mass graves
of family members and friends.
They barely move, barely speak, barely believe
it's over.
Stunned by their own survival,
they stumble or are carried into a new world order.
Watch their eyes.

***

Summer Marsh

The marsh lies sullen
        under summer's burdens.
Mist hovers, hung between the hills,
And leans on green and browning grass.

The summer-shallow brook
        slides under sun-dried banks,
Barely bothering the roots of water lilies
That knit the whole together.

Beth Ellen Jack
Huntington Beach, CA

With a Click of My Heels

I hold your shoes and close my eyes,
the long pause of your absence
languished all afternoon.
Tissue paper stuffed in heels and purses
seemed unfamiliar.
Your seven metal hangers looked empty and sinister.

Somehow I must find a way back
from this empty closet and rows of elegant shoes.
I must summon the child who remembered to be brave,
like Cinderella,
or that girl from Kansas,
who recognized clues, knew slippers were the answers
to everything, a sure guarantee that one could escape
a fire, a witch, poisoned flowers,
even tragedy.
I stand alone, barefoot.

Gerry Rita Di Gesu
West Chatham, MA

Spring Day

Dangling prisms refract comets of color and hope
across stark walls of my kitchen and heart

The cat stalks a rabbit which becomes
a frozen statue hidden behind red tulips

Squirrels and jays battle at the feeder

The phone—
death of a friend, prayers for my daughter,
my husband's soft voice

Mail—
hope for a cancer patient, birth of a baby

I write—letters, essays, poems

Late rays of sun slant through the window
and form a golden orb of promise
enveloping daffodils in a green bowl

Light rests on forsythia reaching for joy
from a vase in a corner of the room

This beauty existed last spring but was unseen
Today I taste peace.

Carol Luchetti
Thomaston, ME

Proposal: 1957

He must have borrowed the car that we were in
as we were seldom ever in a car, as I recall.
I can't remember even if he brought a ring
when he proposed to me, a high school girl.

Something in me rose up to refuse
although he was quite suitable and may
have made an ideal husband, but to choose
from a small sample at the time was not my way.

Now other men I chose in life to wed
proved not to be my true ideal by far.
I could have done much worse than him: and did;
that guy, that night, in that parked car.

***

Byron Hoot
Wexford, PA

A Private Conversation

Oh, tell me what you
Think as long as you agree
With me, the Devil
Says inside each of us.

Diana Kaufman
Kenilworth, NJ

When the Fire Goes Out

There is nothing left but the crisp smell of burning wood, hot metal, wisps of steam rising slowly from the remains of what used to be our home. I stand in the cold drizzle watching the firemen reload their truck. Emergency lights flash and cast an eerie glow on the houses and trees. Moments ago I came home to see the shiny red trucks in the street, their hoses reaching into the gaping doorway like huge black snakes. My children used to crash noisily through that same doorway after school, calling out to me, "Mom! I'm home! What is there to eat? Can I go over to Emily's house?" Now they are married and on their own.

The roof has collapsed into the first floor. I can barely see the outline of the blackened refrigerator, now leaning slightly toward the scorched and smoking cabinets, their contents reduced to shattered shards of my mother's china and yesterday's groceries. I ponder the loss of my wedding pictures, the favorite comfortable chair I just paid $900 to reupholster, my children's artwork that hung throughout the house, bills and bank statements, old high school yearbooks and college textbooks, my collection of paperback spy novels, the thick biographies of Winston Churchill, John Adams, Thomas Jefferson...all the memorabilia of a 25-year marriage, collected randomly on holidays, family vacations, birthdays, anniversaries...nothing now but ashes and soot.

A neighbor gently places a warm blanket around my shoulders, kindness and compassion pouring from her eyes. I only ever waved at her on the rare occasions we were entering or leaving our driveways at the same time. Suddenly she is my best friend, a shoulder I can lean on, who will hold me while I shiver and cry.

Just at this moment, Joe arrives, races from his car to stand stock-still in the driveway, shock and horror in his

Diana Kaufman
Kenilworth, NJ

eyes as he takes in the total destruction. He is speechless; his shoulders shake. He turns toward me. I scurry into his trembling embrace. He squeezes me so my ribs will break. He says, "Thank God you're all right!"

We stand quietly now watching the scene. My sweet neighbor brings us both a cup of coffee to warm our chilled hands. Even though the fire was hot, the air is frosty and damp. We are both shaking still. There are no words to express the despair, the sadness of watching 25 years of our lives go up in smoke. For now, there is nothing more to do. We talk quietly with the fire chief. What do we do now? Where do we go? We are lucky. We are alive. Our cars are not damaged. We look at each other and take a deep breath. "Well," says Joe, "I guess we can bunk with the kids tonight!" And hand in hand, off we go to break the news to the kids.

***

Janice Babcock
Wauwatosa, WI

Regina

You shared writing words in my youth
Your jubilee, my published poem to see

You brought joy in the cards you sent
You showed gentle leadership

You lived in love
You followed the light

You are in my heart
Your joy lives on

Janice Babcock
Wauwatosa, WI

Majesty of the Plains

O mighty buffalo, in the early days you brought abundance
to your Lakota natives.
Tribes took only what they needed.
They did not abuse the wealth your herd brought to them.
You were the source of nourishment to the Lakota.
They used every part of your body.

I ate your meat in a delicious buffalo burger.
I tested moccasins made from hide.
I wore beautiful jewelry made by a Lakota craftsman who
used your horn for my necklace.
I touched pouches made from your internal organs to hold
treasures.
I heard the steady beat of a drum made from your hide.
I viewed a peace pipe made of your horn that cemented
friendship between different cultures and nationalities.
I admired your hair woven on those magnificent chiefs'
headdresses worn at the Rosebud pow wow.
I experienced your hidden language in Lakota dances at the
pow wow.
I attended Mass with the altar table resting on your
beautiful buffalo fur.
You gave your whole self.

O mighty buffalo, you are the Majesty of the Plains.

Janice Marcopulos
Rockport, ME

Right on Schedule

My alarm,
slashes through my sound of sleep,
like the sensation of snapping glass,
using nothing but your bare hands.
My heart jumps.
It's 5 AM.
Time to travel to the usual place.
New York.

My eyes never open the whole trip there.
I lose track of time,
either listening to music,
or listening to my thoughts.
But when car sickness hits,
It's as if time slowed down just to annoy me.
I challenge myself to not ask the usual question.
"How much longer till we get there?"
I've only succeeded twice so far.

I've reached the destination,
I fall asleep quickly.
As if only seconds passed,
I wake up to my friend,
taking piano lessons next door.
Then,
right on cue,
I hear the ice cream truck's music,
farther,
then closer,
ringing in my ears.
Playing that same song.

(continued)

Janice Marcopulos
Rockport, ME

Over and over again in my mind,
beyond my control.
Remembering those days I ran to my parents,
frantically asking them for money.
To buy a cold treat,
on a hot day.

***

Lou Roach
Poynette, WI

The Streets

A scrim of fog softens lighted windows,
turning them to segments of saved sunlight,
collected well before the rain began.

Neon signs, curtained by the thickening mist,
become luminous forms, offer no hint
of what they might say, now abstracted by the wet.

Colors gleam along Main Street.
Gaudy halos circle every light,
their softened luster mirrored on the concrete.

November sweeps slowly through the streets,
bearing dark and damp and mystery,
and leaves a landscape of cold brilliance—
the finale before snow.

Zibette Dean
Edgecomb, ME

Main Street

I park close to Paige's Deli
where fry oil, hot pavement
candle scent from somewhere
smell like every seacoast tourist downtown.
I walk by Fisherman's Catch.
Inside the big glass front
Rob in his baseball cap
is wrapping flounder.
I walk away from the bridge
but the river is right there.
Laughing gulls squawk overhead.
A sparrow cheeps under a deck.
There's a line of cold vacationers
outside the Breakfast Place.
A man with his arm in a sling
walks a puppy on a leash.
The DOT redid the sidewalks
wide enough to display garden benches
and marked-down t-shirts.
At Waltz's Drug Store and Bus Stop
morning coffee regulars
line the front counter.
At the top of the street
the big Baptist Church
village landmark and clock
has its steeple off for repairs
resting beside the church
like a top hat on a hall table.

Wesley Reddick
Belfast, ME

The Driver

It's August, a dump day and a hot one by Maine standards. There are two men limbering along in a van with their first load of demolition debris from an old barn they razed the day before. The driver's T-shirt sleeves are torn off at the shoulders and his clothes are dark with sweat, grime and sawdust. The breeze that the windows suck in past the men, through the load of smelly planks, dislocated ants and four by fours, then out the open tailgate doors, isn't doing much to cool them.

The driver's right hand man Gabe; six foot eight and preoccupied, is slugging down a gallon of previously frozen-solid but now warm Yerba Maté. He's edgy, uncomfortable and is completely drenched as if by an upended cow trough. The driver thinks out loud about a cup of coffee. Gabe unwedges his knees from the dash where there should be a glove compartment, and shifts his long folded body to face away from the driver. He settles into the new position with his head out the window, "You are a sick man," he says with eyes closed, lifting his chin to the wind, his mop of hair fluttering a clean spot into the side of the van.

Before going to the dump, they head downstreet to the waterfront, pull into the Fuel and Coal Company yard and ease onto the truck scale. The stately granite building is generally dedicated to matters of fuel oil, propane and coal, but the driver isn't there about that, he burns wood mostly, though less of it these years, on account of it getting too troublesome to haul and split himself. Inside the sunny office, a grey metal box mounted between two grand windows, jumps alive with a series of authoritative ka-chunks, stamping the weight of the van when empty (the tare established a few days prior), the weight of the van as it sits presently, and then the calculated weight of the load itself onto a 4 x 6 oak-tag card, so the attendant at the dump, three miles away, will know how much to charge for the load, taking the fine art of guessing weight of demolition debris, out of the argument. A five-dollar convenience fee is charged by the Fuel and Coal Company for the stamping service.

A man in a clean white shirt stands behind an occupation-segregating, room-partitioning service counter, and with rubescent fingers, tugs a limp five dollar bill from the driver's brown hand and lays it in the drawer of a handsomely restored cash register. It goes, "chick-dingggg."

"For what they're gettin' at the dump, it'll cost what you make building a new one, to throw the old one away...is what it's like these days," says the owner's son, a different man in a white shirt and tie, with short groomed hair, black as crude oil. He's sitting on a desk like he's in a Newport 100's ad. He doesn't have a cigarette, but two fingers of his hand, placed on the round of his knee, are posed in reserve. The driver wants to say, that for what it costs to heat a house with oil these days he could build a new one too, but he doesn't. That's too many building projects in one day for an old guy and tearing things down is where he's at now anyway.

The air conditioning is blowing so cold it would make February seagulls squint, and the skin on the driver's arms is starting to hurt. He snatches up the stamped card when it's slid across the cool metal counter, the surface of which has worn to silver grey, further burnishing the line between those in the right line of work and the unfortunates. The driver notices the secretary in the office down the hall, sitting in a shaft of sunlight at a computer, is wearing a grey fuzzy sweater. The two men are in long sleeve shirts and that one, in a damned tie, his pointy Adam's apple, set like a trophy in the powder dry pinch of his collar. The driver recalls visiting this office during the winter concerning the smell of propane coming from a new neighbor's vacant property, and everyone was in short sleeves, the secretary in a sleeveless dress. The driver knew that if it were this cold in here then, they would have turned the damned heat up, and had one of their so-called technicians check the boiler.

"Thank you, Roy," the driver says to the first white shirt, then, "...little warm in here, in' it?"

"Better than workin' out there in that," Roy says flatly with a peculiar smile that leaves a chunk of frigid air like a fish tank full of ice cubes, idling over the counter between him and the driver.

"You're welcome," the owner's son says, correcting Roy's customer etiquette, then gestures toward the thermostat with a wave of his hand like he's lobbing an ash into an ash-tray, "Check the AC would you, Roy?" he says with a proprietary hue as cool as menthol smoke rings.

The driver squints up at the air conditioning vent, gives the stamped card a sniff and heads outside where a wave of heat exhausts him for an instant, but causes the lingering scent of the fresh ink to bloom in his nostrils.

In the few steps it takes to return to the van, the driver leaves on a momentary journey back to an auto service garage where he worked sweeping the floor and pumping gas for a few summers when he was young. The garage was spacious, with most of the light coming from the rows of windows in the four bay doors. Three cars usually up on lifts, their undercarriages showing like private parts, and two on the floor. Three mechanics in blue-grey coveralls worked on several cars at the same time, rolling wooden carts of neatly arranged tools to where they were needed. There was a constant din of hissing and banging, and the staccato clicking of socket wrenches chipped at the ears. The air was acrid with smells from flame cut steel, crank-case oil, vulcanized rubber, and gasoline, the concoction of which, would infuse clothing through to the skin, causing boys and men to become addicted to it.

All around were neatly stacked columns of tires, dog-legged exhaust pipes, meticulously organized V belts, racks of skinny copper tubing and walls of shelving, crammed with

Wesley Reddick
Belfast, ME

boxes of automobile parts from large to tiny. Here and there were grinders, drill presses, air hoses and a few machines designed to do very specialized mechanical jobs. And every thing, every where, was subject to a constant precipitation of greyness.

On the floor against a wall, there was a large, half-round foot-lever activated sink. Beside it, was an impressive oak desk, blackened by ten thousand handprints, and profusely spotted on one side with Boraxo hand soap. Above the desk, the darkened bead-board wall was home to no less than twelve dozen keys on rings hanging on nails and brass cup hooks; singles, doubles, triples, some new and some having been there since the present co-owner's father, Art Pearce, opened the place in 1924.

Under the desk, on a shelf where there should have been a drawer, sat an oil stained, wooden Vermont Maid cheese box, emptied of it's comestible slab some decades before, but since has been found to be the perfect size to hold key tags. They were large for their purpose and had white strings looped through reinforced holes in one end. Mr. Art Pearce himself took an old key off a nail and in trembling concentration, tied a tag to it. "That key is damned near old as I am," he said, then opened a black tin box on the desk that housed a large ink pad and a handsome, burgundy handled rubber stamp. He pounded the stamp in the ink, then pounded the stamp on the key tag with practiced precision. PEARCE GARAGE the sporty Chevy logo boasted in smudgeless blue and under the logo it read, *"Your Chevy dealer—we're always here."* Mr. Pearce held the key tag to his nose for a good whiff of the fresh ink, snapped the stamp box closed then tapped the boy's chest at his heart with two boney fingers, rigid as trunnion pins, "You have something special in there son, take my word for it. Now I want you to take this key...and go out and see if you can start something on your own with it." He gave the key to the boy, who followed old Mr. Pearce's lead (as he often did) and put the tag to his own nose as well, drawing in the chemical fragrance. It smelled like the printed paper from the mimeograph machine at his school. Later that day, the young Mr. Pearce, in exercising his new role as co-owner, took the boy aside and informed him that his services were no longer required. Later that week, the aged Mr. Pearce fell ill and never returned to the old garage.

In the van, the driver fans the scale ticket at Gabe who's reading lines from the script of a play he is in and whispering them back to himself. His blinking eyes roll to the driver, "Thanks, that's really helping, I'd swear it's only a hundred and eleven in here now." The driver curls the card into a square hole in the dash where there should be an ash tray, then drives the van off the platform's hefty planks and teeters towards the dump. Gabe leans out his window again, holding his elbow up to catch air in his armpit, "Eez too vahhm," he says, "mine beautivol bodee ees meldingg-k."

"What's your guess?" The driver asks, flicking a thick and dirty finger at the scale ticket.

"Espresso shake if I'm within fifty pounds," Gabe says and recites a few lines out the window.

"Hell," says the driver, "extra thick mocha double shot if you're within half a ton. It's too hot to be taking any chances. I'd be joining you this time."

Gabe replies feigning insult, "You sir, have the faith of a black fly. Fifty pounds," then turns to size up the load, tilting his head in mental calculation. Shortly he says, "Eight hundred...and fifty, no, eight hundred seventy five. No eight eighty. Eight...eighty-eight. What is...eight hundred and eighty-eight pounds.... Tre-nack has spoken."

"I think you mean Carnak," the driver says, "Jonny Carson, The Tonight Show."

"Jeopardy, Alex Trebek/Carnak...hybrid," Gabe says.

"Touché," the driver concedes and pulls out the scale ticket to look at the total. "Let's see how far off my thespian apprentice is this time, or are there shakes in our future?"

Wesley Reddick
Belfast, ME

The driver holds the ticket at arms length for better focus. It trembles a bit in his hand. The number at the line, *net weight,* reads, an uncanny, 888 pounds. The driver hits the brakes. Their load heels up and settles. A car behind them delivers a perturbed beep to their open tailgate and pulls around cautiously, waving an arm, the horn beeper's mouth contorts in hostile spasms of air conditioned silence behind his rolled up windows. Gabe is clearly puzzled. The driver smacks Gabe's arm with the backs of his fingers,

"Why, you hawt shit..." he says grinning, with some parts of the words leaking out where there should be teeth. Gabe's really never guessed within four-hundred pounds and he's been on the awkward side of practical jokes too many times, he takes the ticket, curious and skeptical...but hopeful. Why, he's not sure, eight-eighty-eight is an unlikely number. He reads the card out loud. A look of shock and delight comes over his face like he was just sprayed with a garden hose. He bellows his favorite profanity that he saves for special occasions, something Latin sounding that he loosely transcribed off a municipal building in Augusta, which he believes leans heavily toward the irreverently sexual side of classical stoicism. Then he does James Earl Jones as a Baptist preacher, "The gods of all things great and small made of wood and nails and tar that are to be discarded, crushed and burned, are with us. Hear me brothers and sisters, there is a divine presence in our midst today that speaks through this humble servant, Gabe.. of Nothingham!"

Gabe puts the card to his nose and draws the ink into his nostrils as if it's perfume, then exhales, becoming Robert Duvall, "Ahhhhh...I love the smell of tonnage in the morning. It reminds me of victory!"

The driver says, "Clint Eastwood wasn't in Apocolypse Now. That sounded like Clint Eastwood," and puts the van in park.

"Hey, Clint is close enough, it's hot out. No one can do Robert Duval anyway. And don't rain on my parade, you old

Wesley Reddick
Belfast, ME

hoot," Gabe says.

The driver leans forward fishing for something on the dash which is festooned with stuff and bears a striking resemblance to the crescent beach at the end of the harbor after a good storm; Moxie cans, fishing gear, plastic bottles, to-go containers, a busted pot buoy, prickly blue rope, tools, rusty pipe, a sprawling collection of old nails, rings of keys, invoice pads, engine parts, measuring tapes, rust stained anthropomorphic driftwood, oarlocks, brown frozen chain, nuts, bolts and rocks. He goes at it with both hands knocking overflow onto the heap already on the passenger side floor and finally pulls out a rusted and bent 30-penny square-cut nail. The driver gestures to Gabe for the ticket, Gabe hands it to him smiling.

"This antique nail's only about twice as old as I am. You realize that?" the driver says holding it up like it's that one glass of well aged single malt scotch he's ever had.

"Yeah, that's pretty old...kinda cool," Gabe says, appreciating the perspective.

A pick-up truck pulls up beside them, "Everything okay?"

"Just getting some paperwork done, my em-*ploy*-ee just quit," the driver says.

"I didn't quit." Gabe says, keeping his smile on, and tries to size up what was going on. He's heard the driver talk crazy plenty times before.

"Funny place to do your biz'niz in'it, Bub?" the pick-up says.

"Not so funny," the driver says and lays his arms out wide as if presenting the cab of his truck to a game show contestant, "I do all my business in my office. Now if you'll excuse us."

"What the hell was that?" Gabe asks.

"How long you been worken' for me Gabe?," the driver asks while stitching the nail into the ticket like a pin through an award ribbon.

Wesley Reddick
Belfast, ME

"Three years this past April...pretty sure," Gabe says, still amazed at his lucky guess but watching the driver curiously.

"Well, my friend..." the driver says, "I'm afraid I'm going ta...have to let you go."

"Are you serious?" Gabe says, his face going straight now.

"Serious as a heart attack and you're right, you didn't quit...I'm firing you," the driver answers. "What you need to do is to take this award and go start something with it. Build something real with that nail, why don't you." He hands Gabe his award and firmly pushes him out the door. The driver's arms are forceful as a log-splitter when he needs them to be.

"But....my cars at your place..." Gabe says stalling for time, his unlaced workboots touching down on the hot pavement. Beach stones and a bent screwdriver exit onto the road with him, a spool of corroded wire drops and rolls awkwardly past his big feet into a dry ditch.

"You can't really call that heap of deb-bris on wheels a car...and it's mine anyway," the driver says, "and you only live...." he points across the harbor to a cluster of crooked white houses clinging to the shore, "...just over theya."

"Is that what this is about, that pig pen of a car?" Gabe says like he's figured it out, and tugs his pants up.

"Doesn't have a thing to do with it, you can have it if you want to. Come by the house and get it and we'll even-up for the week,"

"And last week!" Gabe shouts.

"And last week," the driver says and has to lean over onto the empty seat and crank his neck in order to catch Gabe's lofty bright grey eyes. "You're a good kid, Gabe. Now listen, you don't have a stamp on your forehead that tells everybody what you're worth or what you have to be...but you will if you keep on with me...even another minute. There are plenty of choices out there for someone like you. Now go on...make

Wesley Reddick
Belfast, ME

some choices. You're fired." The driver puts the van in gear and watches Gabe in the side view mirror arch his strapping arms outward as if he were holding the whole crazy world against his chest and shaking it. The driver heads to the dump with the passenger door open, pumping the brakes to bounce it closed.

***

Mary Lyons
Biddeford, ME

Now Come

Now come the days of glory—
Flame on the trees,
The leaves of many colors,
Yellow of exaltation,
Music to my eyes.

Clouds depending from the sky,
Leaves scudding in the wind,
A full harvest moon.

Leaves skittering on cobblestones.
Pale glow of a small maple
In early light
Before the house.

Zibette Dean
Edgecomb, ME

Phoebe's Nest

Around the doorway
of the little cabin
mosquitoes and deerflies prospect
as ever in June.

Over the room where notebooks
mouldered on a bare table
there's a new dry roof.

We're painting the mended clapboards
preparing to celebrate
naturalist Beston's work
on this northern farm.

Tucked under the eaves
a phoebe's nest
holds four speckled eggs.

We paint around the nest
knowing that Beston
would have done the same

hoping the mother will return.

Betty J. Paine
Asheville, NC

Washed Secrets

Gravel crunches under my feet as I walk reluctantly towards the small gray cottage where my grandmother once lived, the odor of pine sap pungent. Tall trees whisper to one another, send an alert of my presence. The wind slaps against my skirt, tangles my hair.

As I approach the house the walls begin to swell unable to contain the secrets they hold. I stand on the doorstep as a cold mist surrounds me, encloses me as if in an envelope. I want to escape, return to my comfortable world. But I am the surviving member of her family. Her house is now mine.

I think about when I was here so many years ago. I try to remember my grandmother, solidly built, feet planted firmly in her black laced shoes, pure white hair braided and wound tightly around her head, gray steely eyes, and thin lips which never smiled.

She lived simply with sparse furnishings, everything orderly in assigned spaces. Books lined every wall from floor to ceiling, each wrapped in plain brown paper covers. No one was ever allowed to touch them. I look at them now and wonder if they explain my grandmother who never made cookies, never held me on her lap, never read me stories. Perhaps they would reveal why my grandfather disappeared when my father was still a child, why my mother became ill in her mother-in-law's presence.

I make myself a cup of green tea from carefully wrapped bags in a square tin box. Wood is stacked near the black iron stove. Small sticks and logs inside are ready to be lit.

My hands tingle as I reach for the first book. The tiny black script flows across the page in familiar letters which spell words I am unable to comprehend. As I try to focus on their meaning they begin to wash from the surface, dribble down the page, drop like miniature rain drops into puddles on the floor leaving the plain white paper garishly bright. I think the evening shadows are deceiving me.

But there is nothing unreal about the now damp braided rug as the words keep falling while I turn page after page. I flip them faster and faster, a shower of words splattering against the floor, water everywhere as I stand on a chair, my soggy suede shoes making dark splotches on the flame stitched cushion. I grab book after book, hold open the covers, watch the storm of syllables thunder and crack like lightening as they fall across the room. The flood of words seeps toward the door, rushes down the steps, is now a waterfall destroying the path to my grandmother's house.

I yank books from the shelves, no longer open them for the minute I touch them they begin to cry their secrets which run down my arms, my legs, across my feet. I am washed away as clearly as the words in my grandmother's books.

***

I only remember that day in brief flickering moments as I sit beside the fire trying to keep warm. A cold damp mist remains inside this dark house at the end of the lane where my grandmother once lived.

I look at the books covered with plain brown paper, stare at their blank pages, and try to remember why I am here.

Maude Olsen
South Bristol, ME

A Moving Picture

Very early on a June morning in 1973 we set out from our home in northern New Jersey bound for our first summer cottage in Maine. In a new GMC Suburban were Bill and myself, our youngest son, a 14 year old neighbor's son, two Airedales and a goldfish. Trailing behind us was a brand new bright orange U-Haul-It type trailer we had bought and packed to the gills with household goods and furniture.

As we started down the long hill on Route 84 between Cheshire and Southington, Connecticut, it was around six o'clock and a fine rain had begun to fall. Suddenly the trailer started fish-tailing wildly out of control. (Due, we later found out, to the weld breaking underneath where the hitch bar was attached.) We were approaching a concrete bridge abutment and as Bill held on as best he could, we went up on the grass, down under the overpass and the trailer then careened up the grassy hill on the other side, pulling the car over as it broke loose and sent us spinning down the middle of the highway upside down.

When we finally came to rest we were hanging from our seatbelts; one dog had bolted through a broken rear window and a couple of friendly truckers, fire extinguishers in hand, were looking in our windows. As they began to help us out we realized that, other than a few scratches, no one was hurt! Including the goldfish! At 6:30 A.M. we were in a huddle in the middle of a rainy highway thanking God, who was very real indeed!!!

Herb Coursen
Brunswick, ME

Learning Physics I

The professor stood on a chair on top of the dark
table—a sarcophagus—in the physics lab,
and held the ten-pound brass weight to his chin.
It was attached to a wire strung from the center of
the ceiling. He let the brass weight go. It zinged
across the room, over the heads of a hundred
undergraduates and toward the far
side of the dishlike space, where chairs were close
to the ceiling there. A lad known only as Fat
Matt looked up and saw the brass reaching
its apogee. He gave the weight a push
with a pudgy hand. The brass swung back across
the room toward the professor, who stood within
the full confidence of his hypothesis.
His eyes grew wide for an instant as the weight
struck him in the side of the face. The chair toppled.
His tweed jacket erased a few equations
on the board behind him as he disappeared.
A hundred undergraduates sat there
appalled at the pendulum's revenge against
scientific certainty. He rose,
the professor did, and stared at the delighted swing
of the weight, brassy and bright in the morning light.
"A room of this shape can produce some strange
convection currents," he said, and we wrote down,
in our notes, "Be careful of convection currents,
whatever the hell convection currents are."

Edie M. Schmoll
Sun City, CA

Sonnet for Spring

Let me be as a quiet stream,

running through your soul—

singing you a melody

timeless and clear—

lacing the edges

of your serenity—

listening gently

for your softest word;

    sharing your happiness—

    with a corner in your heart.

Adding to your wildness,

quickening your heartbeat

    —and smoothing the stones

    that fall in your shadow.

Earl Weigelt
Winslow, ME

Timbercraft

Art as ancient as survival itself—
wily, hair-faced disciples of timberland and waterways,
using wit and wisdom to capture that superlative fur
and meat, leather and oil, and unmatched way of life!
A fantastic pursuit fraught with danger and risk that
opened a continent and founded the fledgling economy
that prospered two nations.

"Coureurs De Bois," woodsrunners, consummate masters
of mountains and flats, rivers and bogs
in search of Castor Canadensis.
Mighty men who read a stretch of forest floor, set of rapids,
breadth of sky with supernatural skill—
keen interpreters of cosmic revelation earthbound,
packing sidelock and tomahawk, snarewire, Newhouse,
Blake and Lamb.

Backbone of a nation, made up of heroes and villains,
champions and cheaters—loved and hated by native and
newcomer alike.
Kenton and Crockett and Bridger and Boone—
fabled, iconic forbears of a land known for freedom.
Would that we still had some just like them
in a day of obnoxious entitlement,
egregious ignorance,
and mind numbing entertainment.

Earl Weigelt
Winslow, ME

But their spirit is not dead, no, it lives on still
in modern-day trappers and trekkers and hunters who take to the forests
even this Fall, with canoe and pack-basket, wool and waders,
nourished in the same solitude, fascinated by the same anticipation
that captured those trailblazers and traders of yesteryear.
“What’s around the next bend?” Or, “What’s up this stream?
or beyond the next pass?” still fascinates one hardy minority!

***

Patrick T. Randolph
Murphysboro, IL

Cloud Curiosity

A cloud presses
Her soft misty ear
To the ground,

Listening to earthworms
Dream of rain.

James McKenna
Hallowell, ME

His Retirement Party

Now it's past midnight but the speakers
keep coming. Is that my father striding
to the podium? Isn't he dead?

He begins with funny stories about my
youth. Then looks sternly at me.
"Son, I know you never forgave me.

But why not answer my letters?"
And who's that next in line? It looks
like Amy Farrell, except she's still

a young woman. Why is she here?
I haven't seen her since 1975, when she
stopped the car and forced me out.

***

Lawyer at Real Estate Closing

And it occurs to him that he also
is a home sold too many times.

Perhaps the new name on his mortgage
is Jealousy or Friendship Neglected.

That's his basement sill nearly rotted or
the roof that's been secretly leaking.

Why didn't he notice the punk wood?
Why didn't he climb to the attic and look?

Arthur Kramer
NY, NY

Childhood Chemistry
A Memoir

Sometimes it's hard to believe these events ever existed —the world has changed so much since then. Occasionally my mind aches trying to visualize the details. If it was not for my continued contact with my boyhood friend Jack who is my one link to that dreamlike era, it might seem as if it never happened. The few photographs I still have stir my sense of reality, but I wish I had a video of those times.

Midcentury Brooklyn, early 1950's, when it was easy to grow up immersed in oneself and totally ignorant of the world beyond Coney Island and Prospect Park. I was entering my last year in my expanding cocoon, Public School 217. The school was a three block walk from our small apartment where I lived with my mom, dad, older brother and two younger sisters. We knew most everybody in our four story apartment house and many of the local neighbors and kids whose parks and playgrounds were the streets. The street game that always comes to mind besides stickball was roller skate hockey using sewer covers as the goals. Sticks and hockey pucks were not easy to come by so we fashioned hooks out of wire coat hangers, crumpled up one into a ball and created a game called "Scollo." Trying to hook the "ball" after it was thrown into play by the goalie was difficult, but nowhere near as difficult as trying to wrest it from the opposing team or scoring a goal by heaving it on to the sewer cover. Needless to say we could have used some armor for protection.

Team sports were not my forte. We'd gather around for a game and the captain of each team would alternate choosing teammates from the group. It was not so bad being the last choice, but when the captains had to toss to see whose team I would not be on, I was convinced I didn't have any great sports talent. However, when it came to "scientific" pursuits I shone and could always find somebody to help carry out my devious ideas. Such was the case with Philip who complemented my brains with his brawn and my height with his lack of height, and shared my love of pyrotechnics. We began by dropping fireballs of newspaper off of the roof to startle passersby, then moved on to modest blazes which were usually under control. Soon we achieved a minor conflagration almost reducing the neighborhood garage door to ashes. This brought the partnership abruptly to a halt, however, as Philip's mother severely scolded me for corrupting her innocent son and forbade us to collaborate any more..

David was a different sort of scientific partner. He was interested in more lofty pursuits and was one of my "rich" friends—he lived in a house in a tree lined residential neighborhood. Somehow I convinced him, his mother, and his father to allow us to conduct chemistry experiments in their attic. Chemistry sets in those days contained chemicals that today would have so many warnings on the label you would be afraid to open the bottle. However, we soon grew tired of the many canned experiments in the manual such as "How to turn blue water red," "How to grow purple crystals" or "How to make a yellow, red or green flame." This, we began to realize, was not what young clever scientists such as ourselves should be spending their time doing. We needed more creative scenarios, something more dramatic.

We started with glass bending and blowing but after some curly tubes, a few bubbles, and some charred fingers we lost interest. We searched around the house for chemicals with cautious labels. The kitchen yielded lye or sodium hydroxide and we soon discovered why you should always add the lye to the water and not vice versa. A lot of noise and heat and bubbles were what the caution was all about, not to mention a few ruined pots and pans. We were on the road to knowledge.

Rubbing alcohol provided great fuel for a flame thrower

idea. Veto spray was a deodorant that came in a palm sized plastic squeeze bottle. We filled an empty Veto spray bottle with alcohol, held a lighter flame or lit match at the nozzle and fired the contents. Didn't always work though. Sometimes the spray force doused the flame, and it's a good thing, otherwise poor Sheldon, who we tried it out on, would've faired worse than just hot alcohol in his eye and we might have been thwarted forever in our scientific endeavors instead of just severely reprimanded by David's parents.

Wooden matches, in those days, had both red phosphorus and the more flammable white phosphorus on the tip. They could be struck anywhere, and that we did, including on many parts of our anatomy. Very carefully, we filed the tips of hundreds of matches producing an abundant supply of red but, more interesting, white phosphorus which was not available anywhere. Now we were adding some potency to our chemical supply. A few flare ups later and we quickly learned the need to mix in caution with our chemicals. Good scientists should have some control over their results, which we began to, however, there were mistakes.

We began to research books for new ideas and our efforts revealed that we needed chemicals not supplied in our set or in local stores. We found a place called New York Scientific Supply in Manhattan that was on the second floor of an old commercial building on East 11th Street. These places could never exist today given the amount of protection and caution authorities feel compelled to surround our everyday lives with. Up the creeky wooden stairs we walked through a big wooden door and suddenly found ourselves in a wonderful warehouse lined with shelves and cabinets loaded with bottles and containers everywhere which filled the murky air with indescribable smells. We had been transported to a mysterious den of prohibitive potions waiting to be discovered. As we wandered around we were aware of the eyes of the two surly salesman and their customers bearing in on us. We tried to feign that we knew what each chemical was

Arthur Kramer
NY, NY

for and that we were seriously considering what to purchase for our laboratory but we didn't fool anybody. When our turn at the counter came we presented our list containing among other items sulfuric, nitric and hydrochloric acids. The salesman warily studied the items on the sheet. "I see you have listed here some strong acids. Just exactly what do you want to do with these acids?" came his stern inquiry. I bravely offered an answer. "We need to show how different acids can be neutralized with different bases for a demonstration project in a science fair at our school," was my quick reply. To our surprise, the answer met with approval and, we think, even a little encouragement. We were admitted into the secret club! After that first visit we had little problem getting most chemicals except for some which were definitely restricted.

We now had the means to embark on great new chemical adventures such as: oxidizing marble with hydrochloric acid, dissolving almost anything including gold with aqua regia or nitrohydrochoric acid, dropping small pieces of pure sodium into water and watching it burst into flame and sometimes explode, and etching our names in glass with hydrofluoric acid. Nothing intrigued us more, however, than our discovery of how simple it was to make gunpowder—just mix sulfur, charcoal and potassium nitrate, which were all easily obtainable. Explosions did not interest us but rockets seized our imagination as they did the country at that time and we were determined to have a successful launch.

Model planes and cars in those days were propelled by small steel CO^2 capsules which were sold in any hobby shop. We emptied the capsules, filled them with gunpowder, inserted a gunpowder fuse into the little hole and set up an aluminum tube as a launcher. We were ready to go. Our first attempt was a bit too anxious. We set the launcher up so it protruded out the third story window. Luckily the fuse went out and nothing happened.

After experimenting with the gunpowder mixture we soon

Arthur Kramer
NY, NY

developed an effective fuse but the next few attempts, still out the window, did little more than just fizzle with little propulsion. We began to experiment with the gunpowder mixture and the amount we put in the capsule until finally to our amazement the thing left the tube and landed somewhere in front of the house. I have no idea where David's parents were while all this was going on. We were now ready for a major launching somewhere in an open area; however, such places were not easy to find in the developed streets of Brooklyn. Then it dawned on us that a few blocks away down a dead end street rising up from the underground were the BMT subway tracks. This was the perfect location.

We chose a moonless dark fall night, prepared several of our homemade rockets and fuses, and concealed them along with gunpowder, matches, the aluminum tube and some wood to support the launcher, in some bags. We quietly left the house, took our apparatus and proceeded to the cul de sac. "Do you think anybody saw us?" David asked me. "Nah, we're fine" was my curt reply. We walked silently and looked all around but there was nobody in sight. As we approached the dead end street we could see the one and two story private houses on either side. All was quiet along the tree lined block and we carefully proceeded. The subway tracks at the end were just about at ground level and rose slowly toward Coney Island in the south, becoming an elevated structure about a mile away. Alongside the tracks was a stone embankment a few feet high with a wire fence on top to prevent entry. The embankment made a perfect resting platform for our launcher which we further buttressed with the wood to firmly support it. The projectile path was aimed directly across the tracks at about a 45 degree angle above the ground for maximum distance.

We loaded the tube with the rocket and I said to David: "I think we should pack in some more gunpowder to be sure it doesn't fizzle." David did not hesitate to follow my orders. We then made sure there was a big tree nearby from which to

Arthur Kramer
NY, NY

safely observe the launch. David whispered: "Okay to light the fuse?" "Yeh go ahead." "I'm gonna hide behind that tree right after I light it, so you make sure it's okay," came David's last request. David lit the fuse, I watched it to see that it was burning well and ran next to David behind the tree. Something told us not to look until the rocket was airborne which proved propitious. Before we knew it we were racing away from the scene as doors and windows of the neighboring houses flew open. We were shaking and scared and hoping no one recognized us. The explosion was so loud that the tree vibrated from the shock wave. We felt all over our bodies to make sure our parts were intact. We must have run a mile before we calmed down and realized that we had escaped unscathed and without being detected. Maybe we shouldn't have added that extra gunpowder. We decided to split up and go home to reassess our chemical careers. The next day all we found were some wooden pieces scattered around the launch site and about ten feet away a twisted piece of aluminum.

There were few experiments after the subway bomb. It seemed to serve as an omen for us to direct our energies toward more fruitful and less risky pursuits. As winter closed in I found myself in a quieter cerebral setting playing Pinochle or Bridge every weekend with my less scientific buddies Jack and Frank, risking only my pocketbook. Many years later I ran into David in, of all places, a subway station. He was a salesman selling drugs, I think, or was it chemicals.

Judith Thyng
South Portland, ME

Old Man of the Mountain

An epitaph to New Hampshire's famous granite face of the White Mountains

I am a heap of rocks
But once I was magnificent
Crowds from all over the world
Came to visit me

Indians found me as history claims
Keeper of the white mountain pass
Was my reason for being

The valley was peaceful then
Only a few knew I was there

How proud and invincible I was
A stone face on the mountain
Centuries of guarding
My lofty domain

Years pass and the quiet ends
The teeming throngs
Descend upon me
Their trampled feet upon my brow

Cracks etch across my time worn face
Many tried to save me
But wired jaw and bolted brow
Could not keep me whole

I tumbled in the night
So I wouldn't awaken you
No need to frighten when you die

Judith Thyng
South Portland, ME

Tired and broken
I guard no more
Pieces of my legacy
Now rest upon the forest floor

Though I am a heap of rocks, I have not gone
My stone face
Belays my mountain loft
As in all things, my spirit lives
For those who believe in godly things

***

Sally Belenardo
Branford, CT

Widower's Lament

Little I dreamed, as moonlight brushed your hair,
of when it cannot reach your pillow, there,
where trees embroider shadows on your bed
and breezes tear apart the fragile thread,
where rain's fine needles patiently repair
the edges of the quilt of grass you wear.
As robins weave a chord of song, I try
to raise the shade to wake you, though you lie
aware of neither night nor morning sun.
Your work is finished, and my world undone.

Phillip W. Pendleton
Camden, ME & Melrose, MA

Waking Up Early

All too often I wake up two hours before my intended time. I finally figured out that this early hour was the time I rose when I was working just a few years ago. Okay, so it was more than a few years ago. It isn't that I'm self-conscious about age, though I did claim to be 39 for quite a few years until my son turned 40.

Now where was I? Oh yes. Waking early. It's my brain that's keeping me awake: planning all kinds of things, reminding myself to go to the dentist, get a haircut, trying to decide what I need to take to the apartment I'll be renting soon, wondering how I am going to dispose of fifty years of acquired possessions, etc.

With all the marvelous developments in medical science, why can't they develop a tiny switch behind the ear that will turn off your brain? And oh, yes, there needs to be a timer so that your brain switches on at the time you want to arise.

It's just occurred to me that before this is published in the *Goose River Anthology,* I should get a patent on my fabulous proposal. By this time next year I fully expect I shall be a millionaire.

Segue

The following should be sung to the tune of *"Edelweiss."*

Sizing down, sizing down. So many things to remember.
T'would be much easier to cope if my age was May
Not December.
Hang onto this? No, throw it away.
Wait, it might be handy some day.
Sizing down, sizing down. The whole thing's
Driving me crazy.
I think I'll take a long, long nap
Till things don't look so spacey.

Marilyn E. Canavan
Waterville, ME

County Man

The land is wild
and reluctant as the spring sun
where my grandfather grew great
blossoms of potatoes
upon which were all eyes,
relying on such superior devices
as his weather vein
which he carried in his
right hip joint.

And when the sky dried
he'd hoe—
until his face was laced
with furrows running rivers
everywhere.

He died,
out
standing
in his field.

Hugh Fox
East Lansing, MI

Thirty Years

Thirty years passing like a week, all
the little kisses and je t'aime/I love you
mornings, noons and dawns, the perfect
brown wool scarf, change my bandages,
find the right x-rays, the right (Alban Berg's
Sieben Frühe Lieder/Seven Early Songs)
concerts rivers whitefish along the
Seine behind Notre Dame, even at eighty
wanting to make it another thirty years,
three hundred, three thousand years.

***

Turning

Turning every hour into a hundred years,
ambiguously uncertain about how many hundreds
I ("Medicine isn't really a science, it's guesswork,
theory, intuition, especially when it comes to
invasive cancer.") have left of snow and rain and
sun skies, Oedipuses and Mendelsohnian Reformation
Symphonies, Happy Birthday (January 27) Mozart
Fiestas, another granddaughter/grandson emerging from
our collective genetic archives, year and day
deaths and rebirths, Dearly Beloved always there
like a combo of grandmothers, mothers, sisters,
        all the best oldetime lovers, oldest friends.

C. Ross Painter
Owls Head, ME

Dreamcatcher

They sat upon an old stone wall and talked
One young, the other sickly bent and old,
A mid-October sun warmed the resting pair,
Turned leaves pink, red, yellow and gold,
Against the tall dark evergreens, in Lincolnville.

They spoke of dreams of yesteryear, forfeiting of many,
A camp built by the water, good times all had had:
Boating, swimming, fishing, hiking, berry picking too
And of family closeness they'd once all shared,
At the cozy log cabin on the cove, at Pitchers Pond.

"T'was my dream," the elder said, "these wooded acres
Would help support our fine vacation place."
Now knowing he could no longer do the work,
A single tear escaped; slid down his weathered face,
Sitting side by side in that sunny quiet forestland.

"My chainsaw hardly made a dent, time was always tight,
With work, an' family, things always needed doin',
Should have had a tractor, if I'd only had the money,"
He sighed, "but time slipped by, somethin' always brewin'."
A woodpecker drilling a dead Beech tree echoed in the air.

His once strong hand reached to clap the other's arm,
"I tell ya'," he counciled "don't live to regret too,
Doin' what you plan'd or wish you'd done, take time to
Do them now, things that's important to you!"
He wisely said, that warm Maine Indian Summer day.

C. Ross Painter
Owls Head, ME

The spring no longer in his step, walking a wooded trail.
"I wish," he said with sadness, resting by a big pine tree,
"I'd worked these woods to make them pay, but now,"
He slowly shook his head, "it's just too late for me,
Others now may need to do my job, here in Lincolnville."

And so it was, the younger caught the old man's dream,
The days and years that followed, he tackled the work at
hand,
With new tractor, truck, chainsaw, axe, and sweating toil,
For two decades plus he worked to keep that cherished
land,
And lakeside cozy log cabin, in the town of Lincolnville.

Manny Fiori
San Francisco, CA

Zatanna

They walk in through shadows
beneath window markers, brightly lit with
letters burned out
no one ever reads such
garish welcome signs
to your health and wealth as if
they were genetic stimulants to
everyone who walks
in just beneath the misspelled words
'Psychic Reader Adviser'

Such windows are always neon
glowing, front doors
curiously open

A keen steady eye will perceive
people entering the premises
while keenly discerning,
even fewer are leaving.

Carol Kramer
NY, NY

Mind Over Mountain

The transceiver was sending out its radio signal and beeping, a frightening alert to all involved. Ten skiers tried to locate its position in the deep powder. The group tromped around the vicinity paying close attention to the strength of our own signals by listening intently in the pure silence, the kind of quiet that you experience in very few places. We were on a snowy mountain, accessible only by helicopter, powerful snowmobile, dogsled or IronMan quads and snowshoes. Avalanche training was conducted in the Cariboos in the Canadian Rockies on the first day of a weeklong adventure of heli-skiing.

It was my husband Arthur's 65th birthday adventure. My two biggest concerns were avalanches and helicopters. But of course, I agreed to go. After all, Arthur was the one who encouraged me on the slopes throughout my long learning curve which lasted at least ten years.

I do love skiing, along with the joy of choosing whether I want to try a groomed trail, some powder or a few bumps for each run. The comforts of "on mountain" toilet facilities, stopping for a break when my legs or ego hurts, and deciding what to have for lunch all add to my pleasure of the experience.

Heli-skiing is off trail skiing accessed by helicopter, not actually jumping from the copter with your skis on. It promises fresh powder for each run with unimaginable and majestic vistas, the feeling of being as close to the sky as you can get with both feet on the earth. It offers no creature comforts, those rewards are found in the lodge after a day in the mountains. You ski where the helicopter takes you, eat lunch on the snow when the lunch helicopter brings it and good luck finding a private place to relieve yourself above the treeline.

Avalanche training was complete when we located our

lost beacon and dug it out of the snow. Fortunate for us, it did not require CPR. I was still not convinced that there would not be an avalanche or that I would not end it all in the fluffy white stuff.

Next it was time to learn about the helicopter. I pondered, what's to learn??? I just don't want to die in a helicopter in a gully in the middle of British Columbia worrying about an avalanche. So I paid attention. First, squat when you see the chopper coming, always watch it carefully, and in case it misjudges scramble out of the way without falling down the mountain. Second, protect your face from the blizzard that will hit you when the copter lands where it should which is precariously close, between the skiers and their equipment on a ledge. Next, make sure that your skis and poles are with everyone else's and out of the way, but not on or off the side of the cliff. And finally, duck your head as you board since the blades never stop turning. Reverse the order when you disembark. Then there were the evacuation instructions, of which I remember nothing. I was convinced that I'd be history if anything went wrong in flight. I passed my training without incident and was happy for my yoga practice which enabled me the flexibility to curl into a compact ball whenever those blades approached.

Our first day skiing brought poor visibility, so we had to be dropped off low on the mountain to ski the trees. Panic ensued. My fear of avalanches and helicopter rides was replaced by a new fear of skiing. I was staring down a slope with a 60° angle. Sweating profusely, my heart began racing. I heard every loud thumping beat inside my chest. It echoed throughout my head. I looked down and through the woods. I really couldn't find a slot through the trees where my skies would fit and still go downhill. It was steeper than anything I had attempted before. Most other skiers, including Arthur, skied down to the designated landing and were waiting for the next copter pickup. I was frozen in my unmade tracks, imagining myself as a macabre ice sculpture. I wondered if anyone would find me at the end of the day still clinging to an evergreen. I heard a voice.

"Carol, are you okay?" Gina asked standing tall at 4'11" and exuding the confidence of someone raised on skis.

Always the stoic, "Sure, but I can't figure out how to get down, can you move the trees apart a bit?"

Gina talked me through each turn, telling me exactly how to maneuver. "See those two trees there, ski to those and then kickturn. Then we'll find your next target..oops wrong word."

"There's not enough room for me to kickturn and I'll never get these skis back on if I take them off." I stabbed the tails of my boards into the powder and found myself in a position of a partially opened jackknife. "Now what?" I maneuvered around to orient my body downhill, but my eyes didn't want to follow.

Every muscle in my body ached from tension, but I struggled through each of Gina's repetitive instructions:

"Face downhill.

"Ski to the two pine trees.

"Breathe."

I finally reached the group feeling embarrassed and in pain. I just wanted to quit skiing for the week or maybe forever.

Hans, an arrogant Scandinavian guide suggested, "Let me ski down to the next landing with you so you won't hold back the group."

Off he skied as I fell derrière downhill in two plus feet of snow. It was impossible to right myself lying helpless like a beached whale.

Hans said "Don't you ever work out?"

I held back the tears and growled "Of course, but we don't have 'pick your butt out of the cement' training in NYC." I hated Hans, he was born with a built in macho ski ego and a matching lack of sensitivity. His cherubic pink face, from too much cold exposure, smirked as he eventual-

Carol Kramer
NY, NY

ly helped me stand up.

His words made me rethink the experience. I became determined to enjoy the week, avoid Hans and forget this horrible first day out. I would overcome the fear. I switched to ski with a slower group (Hans would never guide the "powder intro" class). I took the lunch helicopter back to the lodge when I felt like it, savored all the great "après-ski" baked goodies and gourmet meals and luxuriated with many massages to calm my mind and soothe my aching muscles.

I skied with the "powder intro" group for the duration of the week. Each day the sun shone displaying vast untouched fields of fresh fluffy snow. I was infected with the excitement of fresh tracks. On our final evening, we watched the DVD from the "powder intro" group. The guides were pointing out good powder skiing style and it was me on the screen. Even Hans was impressed. What a high.

Arthur enjoyed the experience that he envisioned and I learned once again: try to make it work and if you can't, then you never have to do it again.

Byron Hoot
Wexford, PA

Just This Sanctuary

Everywhere I walk is sanctuary

Today
        The sun in the trees
The only sermon I'll hear,
The wind and the birds
The only hymns singing
And I a congregation of one
Giving only what I have
To give
Which is myself
As the offering plate of time
Passes by wanting nothing
Less than all I am,
Just as I am on this Sunday
In which no church built
By the hand of man will hold
Me—
        But I have never seen
Any sanctuary compare
To what I see in front of me.

Franklin W. Marshall
Simsbury, CT

Minutes of a Backyard Hour

On terrace chairs of beige and orange strips
And metal tubes we link the chains of life
In sunshine of late afternoon when blues
Of sky and bath look paler than the veins
That welt our hands, and shadow-shrouds conceal
More secrets than a senator's charade.

We are not scholars with a flair for odd
And recondite dismissals of theurgic
Presences and cosmic provenance,
But genii of experience who know
The vainness of our world remoulding thoughts,
Where humankind lays bare uncritical
Dependency on myths of paradise
That breed indifference to the stores of Earth.

Now in half-naked warmth we tie the mind's
Wellbeing to a continuity
Of landscape wholeness and organic trust,
Like river rhythms, like a woodland wave.

Drawn to window well, a crow adopts
Its own reflection in the pane as mate.
Thunk, thunk it raps that other birds reply
With rik-rack choruses as they compete
For worms with green, pituitous insides,
Some squashed beneath the rocker rolls. A white
Opossum's belly levels in tick-tock
The fence line grass along its den-bound track.
A millipede approaches from a gap
Between the border bricks. Flies colonize

(continued)

Franklin W. Marshall
Simsbury, CT

Our carriage of refections, and we say,
Outnumbered by this insect overplus:
“Behold a transient cast of light, where blinks
A rainbow spectrum in a spider’s thread.”

***

Steve Troyanovich
Florence, NJ

Sharon

your lips penetrate the illusory
love letters of my dream
igniting this nocturnal cavity
of lost rainbows
across childhood’s mirror...
opening like a flower
the fragrance of your warmth
becomes my vocabulary to exist—
and tomorrow is born
within your immersing tenderness

Mark Sonnenfeld
East Windsor, NJ

During Drizzle

What
Forms
5
10
%
Of
99
Tenacious
Teletypewriter
Table
Token
Put
down
frowns—

Then unable to find a publisher

Lena M. Fleischhacker
Kalamazoo, MI

The Gift of Myrtle

When we moved into the century-old house named Lady Olivia Gray, we were told that the name was that of a haint. Unlike the general population of haints, there was, in the case of Lady Gray, evidence of truth, which lay in a name carved into the only tombstone in an acre of ground known to be a slave graveyard. Nearby was a small wrought-iron enclosed burial plot of the original owners of the house: Josiah and Sarah Armentrout...Dutch, from some place up North.

Mr. Josiah and Miss Sarah rested on opposite sides of the plot, each with large, identifying headstones nestled in a carpet of myrtle and a surround of waist-high boxwood.

In the slave cemetery, the positioning of countless, unmarked pieces of granite indicated that many nameless souls rested beneath the plots of sunken red earth.

*Unmarked...*except for one small stone with the engraved image of a lamb, reclining above the name, Olivia Gray, with neither the date of birth nor the date of death.

I was eight years old when my family moved to the house in 1947. It was the first and last house that my parents...nomads, dreamers and n'er-do-wells of the first rank would ever own. In eleven years of marriage, they had lived in and been evicted from, or left under duress, twelve places. Lady Gray was habitat number thirteen.

Abandoned for twenty years, Lady Gray was one of only two houses on the three-mile stretch of Copper Road, so named for the coppery color of the clay, Georgia clay. This uphill, downhill, winding road that was often impassable, and the frequent sighting of a woman on the premises, had sentenced the house to isolation and desolation. As a family, we were heirs to both, and the house was a perfect fit for us.

Before Mama and Daddy got the property that nobody

else wanted, the previous owner had bought the house and its seventy-five acres of land for the cost of taxes owed. He gutted Lady Gray for her heart of pine boards and the finely detailed moldings that trimmed her doors and windows, leaving her interior a skeleton of hand-hewed studs that rose sixteen feet to crossbeams supporting the upstairs flooring. The clapboard-shrouded remains were to be cremated, until my father, Rufus McBride, asked to buy her.

But it was actually our mother, Anna Siloam McBride ...the dreamer of dreams...who convinced somebody to loan her the $200 down payment. That bought us a year in the house. Numerous hooks and crooks of fortune and misfortune have stretched McBride ownership of Lady Olivia Gray into the twenty-first century. Thanks to the dreamer, we were the receivers of the shell of myths, realities, old stories, many lies and equal numbers of truth.

Among all the "once upon a times" lay a truth we heard about the woman, Olivia Gray, and that truth seemed not to age or to suffer dispute.

In spring, as Anna McBride planted flowers on the hill, a man named Pater hobbled up the hill and told her that he had grown up in the neighborhood of Copper Road and had played with the Armentrouts' six children, four of whom died in one winter of typhoid fever. According to this man, Pater, a grief-stricken Josiah Armentrout boarded up the back room where they died and for ten years, nobody...not even the children's caretaker, Olivia Gray, entered the room.

As for the slave cemetery where Miss Olivia lay, we were told not to go there. According to my father, slaves were buried in wooden coffins, or no coffins at all, and after eighty odd years, the earth covering each grave had sunk. Even under the weight of a footfall, "A grave can sink to God only knows how deep. And furthermore," he warned us, "both cemeteries are full of every kind of snake that grows in the state of Georgia."

The graveyard was, in fact, a tiny primeval forest of briar

Lena M. Fleischhacker
Kalamazoo, MI

patches, honeysuckle, passion flowers and lanky trees, so tall that their top branches swept away the daylight. Malnourished and choked stems of Baby's Breath drooped over nearly every head stone, the larger granite markers that faced East, the direction from which the Savior would come at the appointed time, the Rapture, to raise the dead.

At the edge of this forest, there was a locust tree, whose bean-shaped pods ripened, turned brown, and dropped to the ground. Inside the pods was a tasty treat and I imagined that the burial sight had been the wilderness where John the Baptist fasted, then feasted on the fruit of this very tree, until Salome demanded his head be served on a platter.

Despite the seen and unseen dangers lurking in the slave cemetery, I secretly visited Miss Olivia Gray with bouquets of myrtle, which wilted within minutes after I placed them before the little lamb.

All the other graves were nothing more than sunken earth; only Olivia Gray assumed a personality and in my imagination, she was dressed in a long flowing robe that never soiled as it swept the ground where she walked.

My visits were happy until I invited my brother, Beau, to go with me to share the joy. Beau was only six. He was scared of snakes, catamounts, falling trees, holes in the ground, the dark, booger bears, and the ghost of Josiah Armentrout, who, according to my father, often stood outside the back room window. Watching us, to make sure we didn't misbehave.

Beau could hardly wait to tell Mama and Daddy that "Lilly goes into both cemeteries and eats stuff out of the locust pods and takes handfuls of myrtle to the tombstone that has that baby lamb drawed on it."

For our parents, mainly Daddy, it was about the hundredth time (he kept count), that he had to warn me that if I didn't stop my "curious" behavior, more specifically visiting dead people...if he heard any more of it, no choice was left him but to take me down to Milledgeville, a threat that would reform the most "curious" and incorrigible child (and many adults) in the state of Georgia.

While I sat in my little chair, looking up at my daddy standing by the mantel piece, he recalled the name of Miss Almajean Hobbs.

"Remember Miss Almajean Hobbs?"

"Yes, sir."

In a past so distant that I had not even been born, Miss Almajean's name had been on a Sunday roster of shut-ins at a local church. The minister and two church ladies, as they did for shut-ins, delivered dinner to Miss Almajean. She met them at the front door, the soul of politeness and gratitude, took the dinner, lifted the napkin covering the fixings and invited them: "Y'all come on in the living room here and make yourselves at home."

Rufus McBride's pausing and parsing would rival the best of Barrymore; and he did both as he shifted position before the mantel piece, lowered his head, raised an eyebrow and never blinked an eye.

"Almajean Hobbs was as naked as a jaybird...on a Sunday...stark naked...not a stitch!"

The metaphor of the naked jaybird made no impact, for I'd never seen a naked jaybird. But I understood "stark naked" as very "curious" behavior, especially in front of a preacher.

"Oh yes," he continued, "the authorities in these matters were notified of the woman's 'curious' behavior; and Miss Almajean Hobbs, who wore her hair cut like a bristle brush and climbed trees like a natural born monkey, and tied tin cans on every peach tree in the orchard, was hauled off kicking...(pauses parses and a steely stare)...to where?"

"Milledgeville?"

"...where she *shot off her mouth* to the *wrong party,* who in the *dead* of night, sneaked into her room and with the *spike heel* of a *black patent leather shoe...*"

A wait now, one that would rival the wait for Godot.

Lena M. Fleischhacker
Kalamazoo, MI

"You want to go down to Milledgeville and have somebody take a high heel shoe to you?"

"No..."

"No, what?"

"No, sir...I do not want to go down..."

"Then you stay out of that cemetery."

IN THE BACK ROOM, BEAU, HERBERT (OUR BABY BROTHER) AND I SLEPT IN TWO IRON BEDS on opposite sides of the room, the boys' bed lengthwise against the window, the favorite look-in post of ole man Armentrout and Olivia Gray, though they never visited us at the same time.

With the moon's light from three oversized windows, panes missing, and neither shade nor curtain to block the moon's passing, shadows and shapes moved about the room in a macabre dance to the music of old-house noises, frogs croaking in the elms, and wild birds calling along Honeysuckle Creek.

Daddy Rufus being the original rule maker, fixed our bedtime at precisely 8 o'clock; and if we didn't fall asleep on time, the next rule was that there was not to be so much noise as that of a pin falling.

Often, one of us...usually it was I...didn't fall asleep at the stroke of eight, for which need I hoarded a stash of biscuits, crackers and brown locust pods, the latter, ill gains got from breaking the rule: STAY OUT OF THAT CEMETERY!

On such a sleepless night, as I sat at the foot of my bed feasting on three locust pods, I heard a thin, high-pitched voice....

In the bed across the room, Herbert was visible. Beau was absent. It was past 8 o'clock! And on the night stand was a quart jar of lightning bugs, another "thou shalt not."

I swished the locust pods under my bed sheet; and as I leaned forward to search the room for Beau, I fell to the floor with a thump louder than the noise of a pin falling, but not loud enough to cover the the return of the thin, high-pitched

Lena M. Fleischhacker
Kalamazoo, MI

voice.

As I scrambled to all-fours, there, straight ahead of me, was a large lump beneath the boys' bed, an area usually reserved for booger bears, whoompus cats and in the right season, a litter of kittens. The lump was about the size of the ordinary booger bear.

As I watched, the booger bear lump stretched into the shape of a boy that was Beau, who said simply, "I just wanted to know."

"Wanted to know what, Beau?" Actually I was quite relieved, though I had a feeling that doomsday was upon us.

"At school, when we say the Lord's Prayer, we say, "Hall-o-wed be thy name. Is 'Hall-o-wed' God's other name?"

"I reckon so; it's in the Bible," I whispered, crawling toward him. "How come you're under the bed? Daddy said..."

"Mr. Armentrout was out there, standing by the window. Is he still there?"

I stood up and made a grand show of checking beyond all the windows for the old man. "Not there. You get back in bed and go to sleep. Daddy said..."

Beau didn't trust me. He crawled from beneath the bed and made his own search of all three windows; and seeing no sign of Josiah Armentrout, he sat on the edge of the bed and opened the lightning bug jar. Several bugs blinked up the sides of the jar, toppled over the rim and flashed around the room.

Oh, what a beautiful sight! We reached out our arms and the bugs lighted on us, as if Beau and I were the where that they wanted to be.

The voice of doom hollered from the next room. "Go to sleep in there. And I don't mean tomorrow."

"Yes sir, Daddy," we answered. And by that time, many lightning bugs had escaped the jar and were swarming in every direction. Hoping to rescue them, Beau reached toward the jar, bumped against the night stand and the jar crashed onto the cement fireplace hearth.

Lena M. Fleischhacker
Kalamazoo, MI

Daddy stormed into the back room, a ridiculously comic figure in undershorts that flapped loosely about his bantam legs.

Beau rose to attention beside the bed; Herbert, still asleep, rolled off the bed and stood beside him.

"*What* in the *name* of *Almajean Hobbs* did you break?"

"The lightning bug jar fell on the cement," Beau's voice trembled, high-pitched.

"And *who* brought bugs in the house?"

"Lilly and Hub."

"As if I could not guess it," exasperation dripping off every word; "and *why* Miss Lilly, did you bring *bugs* in the house?"

"Because," Beau told him, "she just likes to look at them."

"Well," he looked at me, "now that you have *woke up all of creation* (he was the master of exaggeration for effect), have you got enough of *looking* at lightning bugs?"

"Yes," I confessed, as Beau collapsed in a spasm of tears and sank to the floor and Herbert crawled back into bed, still asleep.

And finally, our daddy, babbling his finest blend of cussing, went to the kitchen and returned with two straight chairs and slammed one in each empty corner of the room; and with that act alone, he made more noise than we, altogether, had made in several weeks. We took our seats, knowing they were for us, and Rufus McBride, judge and jury, passed sentence upon us for our crimes against all creation.

He propped himself against the mantel piece, ill-costumed for the task, a pair of undershorts hanging limp down to his knees.

"You sit in these chairs and look at lightning bugs until every last one has fell down dead. If it takes all night. And tomorrow...*both* of you are going to take a trip. Ain't but one place fitting for you. Remember Miss Almajean Hobbs?"

"Yes," we both answered quietly.

"Yes, *what*?"

Lena M. Fleischhacker
Kalamazoo, MI

"Yes, sir, we remember Miss Almajean Hobbs," we said, stifling yawns. There was a touch of disappointment; for the threat of being taken down to Milledgeville had been uttered so often that it was beginning to sound more like a broken promise than a threat.

So, we just sat in our chairs, waiting for him to leave the room, all the time watching scores of lightning bugs escape through missing window panes.

In triumph, Daddy swaggered, underwear flapping, into the next room. Beau left his chair and crawled into bed. Then I made a check beyond the windows to see if any ghosts were lurking about. There was only one and I knew right away who it was. Shrouded in a white gown, the ghost raised its hand "good-night"; and that hand, holding a bouquet of wilted myrtle, was as brown as a locust pod.

e. w. oestreich
Damariscotta, ME

The Meadow Rug

The stretch of meadow grass is tortured
now as early Winter winds with bites of
snow begin their pass.
All touch of color spent from Summer's wild,
if scattered, populace of wayward bloom:
red clover, vetch, the elegant Queen Anne's
Lace and spikes of tall Verbascum that grace
each dawn, each sunset storm.
The worn out meadow rug can only wait.

Deep drifts of snow will soon
accumulate and tired grasses all will
die. There's still a magic left at work
beneath it all: invisible—
until some April rain will wash away all
trace of ice. All Winter long repairs
were being made. Next month, as good as new,
will be unrolled the mended meadow rug. And
birds and game return again to feed.

Peggy Gannon
Palmyra, ME

Big Wind

After a day and a night
of hard snowing—
twelve or fifteen inches on the ground—
sustained notes of a high wind
wake me in the morning.
On this lunar landscape
it has carved and sculpted
what no earthly moon has ever seen.
All across the snow fields
I am sole witness to
impossible images
juxtaposed like illogical dream scenes:
long curved surf
breaking on a smooth shore,
crisp eddies 'round a winterberry bush,
hundreds of nomad tents
pitched on a vast plain,
a bead-strung archipelago,
terrapins and violins,
celebrating cellos.
Winter music,
gift of the wind.

Edie M. Schmoll
Sun City, CA

W H E N ?

WHEN will this world's inhabitants
learn to just get along—
It's tougher to start a war, you know,
than it is to join in song.

WHEN will human beings decide—
enough is enough, make peace!
If the people in charge would only say,
"These wars will have to cease!"

Just ask a mother who's lost a son,
why we always have to fight.
WHEN he's dead, does it really matter
who's wrong, or who was right?

WHEN my sweetheart went to war,
and never returned to me—
I hoped, and coped with the riddle
of why this had to be.

> The soldier who dies will not be forgotten—
> husband, father, or son;
> but the tears of millions are on our hands.
> **WHEN will the madness be done?**

Tom Adamson
Fremont, NE

I Will Wait

I will wait until your footsteps fade.
Kiss the grass you walked on,
Each and every blade.
Then I'll lie back down
And slip into sleep in the shade.
I will wait forever, I won't be afraid.

I will wait until your light has dimmed.
Cup close the candle of you,
Keep the flame within.
Then I'll lie back down
And wait for you to come back again.
I will wait forever, this won't be the end.

I can't start to understand
If this is part of a larger plan.
All I know is I won't let our love go dry.
I can measure memories in years.
I can walk the distance out in tears.
All I know is I can't afford to ask why.

I will wait until your breeze has passed.
Then I'll lie back slowly
In the cool dark grass.
The stars ring out the night,
The moon wears out its mask.
But I will wait forever,
The sorry sky will never have to ask.

Noreen O'Brien
Newcastle, ME

"Who Cooks for You . . . Who Cooks for You Aaalll?"

Standing at the window under the cover of darkness, I have been eavesdropping on the intimate conversation that is taking place outside my window. I can't help myself. There is no hope that I will ever know what is being discussed between the two barred owls, but my guess is that he is whispering sweet nothings into her ear.

'Tis that time of year for these owls—time to select a mate and begin preparations for setting up housekeeping. Too dark to see what is happening out there, I judge from the closeness of the calls and reckon the birds are in the evergreen nearest the dooryard and close to the window. Perhaps they are making use of the roosting box mounted there expressly for them.

I imagine she is standing inside the box. One third heavier than the male, I see her yellow bill slightly raised in a haughtiness, as he attempts to impress her with his whispering. For her eyes only, he is posing, standing straight and tall on a nearby branch, streaked breast puffed up, a feathered leg extended with talons pointing as he shows off the fine tools that he will use to keep her and their offspring well fed as they engage in raising a family in the coming months.

The two large birds, among the most vocal of our owls, are performing a duet of rich hoots and hollers. At times, the birds sound much like monkeys conversing; at other times they share a rather soft maniacal laugh. Their most common and definitive call is, "Who cooks for you . . . who cooks for you aaallll?" Now, however, they exchange low grunts, and an occasional soft bark or an excited "hoooo-waaah."

Perhaps they have been debating the value of a "previously owned" nest site where a family of red-tailed hawks once lived. The male owl likely selected this site in early

Noreen O'Brien
Newcastle, ME

autumn, and it must now meet with her approval. Among other things, she is looking for a location that has some, but not too dense an understory for protection from predators, as well as a good source of food in the immediate vicinity.

A few more minutes of this intimate exchange and all is quiet. Perhaps the pair moved off into the night in the silence of owl flight.

Moments later, I turn on a porch light out back before taking out the dog. Instantly, I see a pair of dark eyes turn toward the light—I have disturbed an owl perched atop the bat house—the birds moved only as far as the backyard. Apparently, this bird is hunting—or I have interrupted some mating ritual—because it remains still, but watching the area of the door.

Within a few moments, unperturbed by the light, the owl drops to the forest floor only to lift up seconds later, long yellowish legs dangling, looking much like the legs of a night heron, talons empty. The bird flies into the darkness beyond the range of the light.

Waiting for the teakettle to boil, I stare out the window into the space where the bird was, feeling awe-inspired over my pre-dawn experience. Then I spot it: a barred owl, looking all superior, perched on a horizontal branch just inside the circle of light. Is it the first owl still hoping to catch the same critter, perhaps in the hopes of impressing its mate, or is it the mate, still waiting to be impressed?

I don't dare reach for binoculars—I am afraid to breathe. I remain still as a rock. Peering out the window, I tick off the key identification points of the grayish-brown barred owl: about 20 inches tall, barring on the feathers of the upper breast to the throat, and below that, a pale breast and underparts heavily streaked with dark, elongated markings. Its round, "earless" head has dark eyes—our only owl with brown eyes—within the well-defined facial disc. The bird's head turns first over its right shoulder, then over its left, as it surveys the ground below its perch. What is it hearing that

Noreen O'Brien
Newcastle, ME

I cannot?

I have moved from eavesdropper to voyeur—and still I cannot stop myself. I know I'll be back tomorrow morning before first light, on the lookout for more intimate exchanges between the barred owl pair. It is my hope that they, too, will be back.

***

Mary Lyons
Biddeford, ME

Thinking of U & Yr Shaggy Body

Thinking of you and your shaggy body,
And Auden's brokers,

Coming upstairs with a bowl of oatmeal,
And my regrets,

And seeing through the narrow window
Sunlight on red shingles,

Next door's ragged house.

Steve Troyanovich
Florence, NJ

one more rainbow for the road

> ***Traces of a future lost***
> ***In between the lines***
> ***One more rainbow for the road***
> **—Kris Kristofferson: *This Old Road***

was it the dream
or the remembrance
of the dream
that was *real...*

detours crisscross
like Rod Serling signposts
inside my mind

the rearview mirror
of fugitive shrouds
the broken recollections
in between the lines
of lost highways

i was alone yet with me
the fading roads of yesterday:

i rejoined Lew Welch for another lifetime
one afternoon in Riverside

near the torn desolation on the banks
of the Ohio James Wright shouted encouragement
to me

i heard Abbie Hoffman's voice again—still calling
me his flowerchild with thorns...

Steve Troyanovich
Florence, NJ

i survive. dreaming... lost...
huddled in corners of memory and frail illusions
as lonely as the darkness
traveling down this road

***

Roslyn Morrill Marcopulos
Rockport, ME

Flightless

All our things are broken. It is time for us to leave.
I am sad, but I know the earth must breathe.
The water came and pulled our feet into the sand.
I am sad, but I know it had nowhere else to go.
The machines spew invisible poison across our land.
I am afraid.

The birds have already flown away
Flightless, we are left behind.

Dianisha Leonard
Worcester, MA

The Visitor

It strips you to the very core,
leaving your wounds exposed to air.
It haunts your every waking moment,
allowing you to do nothing...
Nothing is exactly what you feel like,
when it has consumed all that is good within.
He arrives at your doorstep with bags in tow,
without a phone call or an invitation.
Too late to tell your visitor to leave,
although he has overstayed his welcome.
Not able to escape, you endure,
hoping to one day be free of his presence.

***

Byron Hoot
Wexford, PA

To Have This Inheritance

My parents had so
Little all they
Could give was
Themselves.

Lois A. Hart
Bath, ME

The Beach on a Hot Summer Day

The seashore beckons me one more time. A sandy beach on a hot summer day evokes memories of a more abundant time when life was filled with enormous energy, enthusiasm, and purpose.

My senses are awakened by the fresh, cooling ocean breeze, the heady aroma of salt air, the gentle sound of breaking waves, and the breathtaking beauty of that infinite expanse of water that touches on so many unseen shores.

I take off my shoes and walk gingerly over the hot, dry sand to the water's edge. I wade in cautiously. The frigid water shocks and numbs my feet, and I sink ankle deep into the layers of coarse sand and crushed shells as the waves advance and retreat. Sinking ever more deeply into the layers, a strange feeling of sadness and nostalgia washes over me while I think of how quickly the years of my life have come and gone. I am spooked by a suddenly breaking wave that spews sea spray in all directions. I lick my lips and taste the delicious, familiar saltiness.

Strolling lazily along the water's edge, I stoop occasionally to pick up interesting looking shells and rocks, pieces of frosted sea glass, and scarce, but precious sand dollars of varying sizes. These timeless treasures never seem to lose their appeal.

I turn and scan the beach. This is where I came when I was a child, later brought my own children, and now my grandchildren. Throughout the years the scene has remained the same. Children continue to build sand castles with moats in the hard-packed wet sand, and embellish them with bits of material scavenged from the beach itself, while others dance about in the surf, emitting occasional squeals of laughter as a breaking wave catches them off guard. Little tots clad in tiny bathing suits, and carrying colorful pails and

Lois A. Hart
Bath, ME

shovels, toddle around in the soft, uneven sand.

Sandpipers skitter about, leaving dainty little patterns in the wet sand. Seagulls fly overhead announcing their presence with loud squawks, while others strut boldly amongst the beachgoers, hoping to spot an unattended morsel, and seizing any opportunity they can to snatch food right out of the hands of their startled, unsuspecting victims.

Blankets and brightly colored umbrellas dot the soft, sandy beach, and bronzed, shiny skinned sunbathers soak up the sun's rays. It is obvious that suntans have not gone out of style.

Sitting and looking out over the ocean, and listening to the steady rote of the surf, I am reminded that, like the constant ebb and flow of the tides, life is an ongoing cycle of loss and renewal, and as we become weaker in body, we grow stronger in spirit.

Once again the seashore has worked its magic, drawing me back through the layers of my life, and somehow reassuring me that each layer has meaning, that growing old is all part of God's plan, and all is well in my world.

Liz Moser
Phippsburg, ME & Baltimore, MD

The Chase

I chase the sunset,
peering from the windows of my high-rise eyrie in the city,
see the winter ice-break edge of sun descend
far to the south before I've had my evening drink.
I run from room to room, keeping pace with racing days that grow
from short to long, from south to north, allowing time to savor
dayglow turned to heavy purple, summer stretching sun time.
I run I run from short to long from south to north from year to year
from dark to each new dawn
and wonder that I still enjoy
the chase

Mary Jo Balistreri
Waukesha, WI

Archeology of Desire

Steam curls its way up the spout,
unfurls petals of mist that displace
the winter of a cold kitchen.
My gramma cups her hands around
the blue-willow cup, its glaze
cracked and veined. She lowers
her face to the heat, takes a sip
and rests her head against the back
of the rocker, the hiss of wet wood
our background music. Soon
the stories spin from her mouth,
worn from telling, smooth
as softest flannel. How they tint
the bleak day in warm pastels.
She guides me through the prairies
of youth, the furrowed ground
of growing old, of births and deaths
of children and husband, crocheting
the past with mauve shadows laid
against the gray simplicity
of the North Dakota Plaines.

Susan Marie Murdoch
Tampa, FL

Old Friend

Rain slid in uncertain streams down the blackened pane of the bedroom window, reflecting the amber glow of the candle that burned silently in the corner of the room, giving an abstract effect of poorly crafted stained glass. The storm, in all its fury and fireworks had reached down like long arthritic fingers, and severed the power lines in one swift snap, causing a blanket of darkness to cover the small New England town of Kittery.

I sat on the window seat, nestled contently among the multicolored, hand-stitched pillows and rag dolls that had been passed down throughout the years. I wrapped my knitted shawl securely around me, warm and safe from the angry protest of Mother Nature lashing out just beyond the faded, wallpapered walls and dust-filled velvet drapes.

The flickering flame of the candle gave life and movement to the shadows of the antique dolls that sat upon an old cedar chest directly across the room. The shadows danced, while outside the wind and rain beat loudly against the window, sounding like long drawn out applause in approval of the show.

Gazing around the room, childhood memories leaped out at me from every corner, beckoning me back to much younger years when a night like this would have me shuddering under the covers with my faithful stuffed tiger, named Tiggy, clutched tightly to my chest. So tight, that I swear I could feel its tiny heart beating in fear next to mine. Though losing most of his stuffing and one eye to a tug of war with the next door neighbor's collie and having no fur to mention of from my frequent grooming, Tiggy was my best friend, my companion and my security. We vowed in childhood secrecy to protect each other from whatever dangers lay lurking outside the drafty old cape.

Susan Marie Murdoch
Tampa, FL

My thoughts drifted further to when I was six. It had been just after Thanksgiving on a cold, blustery, winter day and I stood under the archway of the living room. My trusty Tiggy hanging at my side with its hind leg held tightly in my grip. Tiggy looked up at me with his one eye under a floppy paw as if winking and saying, “It’s okay. You can let go. I can finish this somersault, all on my own.”

Across the room, my mother sat in her high, wing-backed chair, her hands moved frantically as if conducting a tiny orchestra in her lap, never losing time while crocheting our new winter hats and mittens. She glanced up at me with a warm, inviting smile and softly asked, “So, Susan, what would you like Santa to bring you this year for Christmas?” I stood there and thought a moment, then looked down at my faded sneakers with their frayed laces toppling out over the worn, wide planked floor. Inside the well-trodden shoe’s, I wiggled my big toe feeling the rough canvas brushing over it through the hole in my sock. My eyes shifted to the friendly grin looking up at me from my side and without hesitation, I lifted Tiggy high in the air and softly uttered, “I want Tiggy to feel better.”

My mother’s hands fell into her lap bringing an end to the silent symphony and a puzzled look swept across her face. Her eyes were fixed on Tiggy and for a brief moment I thought she might burst into laughter at the silly sight of the upside down stuffed tiger dangling from my small pudgy hand. Without a word or even a snicker, she resumed her crocheting and inquired, “Why do you think Tiggy isn’t feeling well?”

I tiptoed across the tiny dim room, lit only by the golden flame of the fire, burning in the stone hearth, and by the crooked floor lamp arching over the well worn chair my mother occupied. I sat down, crossed legged at her feet placing Tiggy securely in my lap. The warm radiance of the flame comforted me as I explained to her with such innocent doubt as to how everyone who came upon my beloved Tiggy, kept commenting on how “sick” he looked and I asked her if there

Susan Marie Murdoch
Tampa, FL

was anything she could do to help my ill-looking friend. She kept on crocheting in silence as I sat there in wonderment at the speed in which she manipulated the yarn around the hooked-shape needle. I was hoping she was thinking of some old fashioned, family remedy for ill-fated Tiggies, when my mother finally spoke and simply stated, "Well, I will see what I can do."

The following weeks dragged but Christmas morning finally had arrived and I awoke in the early darkness. My eyes were still blurred from sleep as I reached out for my soft and tattered Tiggy, but instead I found a hard, furry, fully stuffed Tiger sitting there staring back at me with a pair of bright emerald eyes. I sat up in amazement at the miracle before me, carefully examining the renewed Tiggy, turning it over repeatedly in scrutiny, looking for his missing eye, and bare muslin. I searched for the multitude of restitched seams and bent whiskers, but all were gone the signs of affliction from my old friend and to my surprise; tears began to fill my eyes. This hard, sturdy, brilliant colored tiger wasn't my Tiggy, with its sharp black, vivid stripes and subtle smell of glue like chemicals, similar to the ones found deep within the kitchen cabinet, locked and forbidden to touch. My heart sank and I climbed down from the warmth of my bed, reluctantly grabbing hold of the tail of my unwelcome guest.

I crept softly to the top of the stairs and peered down through the gray haze of all that remained of Christmas eve night, in search of signs of movement in hope that maybe I could still reach Saint Nick before he left and politely request that he return Tiggy to his old, worn out self again.

Anger rose within me as I started down the stairs and I heard the "Thud, Thud, Thud," of the firm new toy banging on the steps behind me. My heart ached for the soft sound and quiet flop of Tiggy.

In the silence of the early morning hour, Saint Nick was no where to be found. I placed the new Tiger on the foot rest of my mother's chair and shuffled slowly to my tiny, wooden rocking chair next to the Christmas tree. Its kaleidoscope of twinkling lights, gave a warm colorful glow to the room, but offered no comfort to the pain I felt for the loss of my friend. I sat in silence, rocking slowly and staring fiercely across the room at the intruder staring back at me and I waited for the house to awaken for Christmas morning.

No amount of comforting or reasoning from my family that day or for many days and months to come, could convince me that I should be happy, that Tiggy was well again. My only response was, "Tiggy's ruined!"

It was years later, while I was exploring in my father's workshop, rummaging through layers of old cloths and paint spattered rags in an old basket, that my eyes fell upon a old familiar face gazing up at me. It was Tiggy. I pulled my old friend from the pile and questioned my father who was working diligently repairing my punctured bicycle tire. I listened in astonishment as he explained to me how they had searched high and low for a second Tiggy that Christmas. When they had found the new stuffed tiger, they hadn't the heart to discard my old, faithful friend.

A flash of light poured through the window accompanied by a loud rumble off in the distance, bringing momentary daylight to the room, and jolting me back from my melancholy past.

With the support of my walking stick, a lengthy, pine colored cane, sanded and polished with an eagle's head carved at the crest, given to me by my son some years ago, I pulled my self slowly to my feet and shuffled across the floor. My knees ached, feeling like rusty old hinges, in need of repair as I made my way to the corner of the room where a collection of various, odd shaped hatboxes lay stacked. I reached up with withered hands, stained with age, and removed the lid of the uppermost box and reached down and pulled from the depths of my past, the old ragged and limp, moth eaten Tiggy.

I turned and climbed up into my four poster bed and

Susan Marie Murdoch
Tampa, FL

pulled the thin, faded blankets up around me and tenderly embraced my days gone by. Peaceful slumber soon came and carried me off to restful, child-like dreams.

***

Peggy Gannon
Palmyra, ME

Bearing Beauty

Crystal beauty,
be graced with flaws.
Traceries of imperfections
give relief from gazing at
the inconceivable, the coldly perfect.
Be laced with nettings,
crazed with cracks,
that we, marred and tinted, may pass
trapeze-like from thread to slender thread.
How else are we to discover
our way through blinding clarity?

Diane Reitz
Winter Park, FL

Brother

When the news came
that you were gone
from the world,

I felt little.

couldn't feel it
until the memories
started flooding in—

an unexpected
rain that flowed
down the mountain

and filled up the
streams with rushing

water, and I remembered
when you knew me
better than anyone,

when you hurt me,
laughing—when
you protected me

from falling—
we laughed about it
until our sides hurt.

Diane Reitz
Winter Park, FL

Then we rolled over
to find ourselves
in completely other
lives

with others
surrounding us
and our memories

a distance so vast,
only your death
could breach it.

***

Patrick T. Randolph
Murphysboro, IL

My Father at Dawn

Farmer's lungs inhale
This morning's purest breath of
A new born May breeze;

It runs inside his flesh, blood—
Overflows into his grin!

Lilli Buck
Bristol, VA

Angel of the Battlefield

It was Fredericksburg, Virginia, in 1862,
Another battle 'twixt the gray and the blue.
The wounded Union soldiers lay on Marye's Hill.
Of running and of killing they had had their fill.

The battle was in a pause; the gunfire had ceased.
The smoke had cleared, but there was still no peace.
Their fellow soldiers had trampled them under their feet.
Their charge had failed, and they were in retreat.

They lay there and moaned before the Confederate wall,
Where only their enemies could hear their call.
They cried for help and begged for water,
These soldiers left over from the slaughter.

They lay there in the snow with their wounds so red,
After all of their comrades-in-arms had fled.
Suddenly a young South Carolina man
Jumped over the wall with a canteen in his hand.

He took water and comfort to the dying Yankee men,
Brave soldiers who would never see home again.
These were his enemies, these men in blue,
Who an hour ago would have run him through.

Christ said, "He who gives a drink of water will have his reward."
This man hardened not his heart, but remembered the Lord.
These suffering, dying, bleeding Northern men,
Their former mortal enemy was now their only friend.

Lilli Buck
Bristol, VA

"Where do you come from, Yankee boy, and what is your
name?"
"My name is Willie Powers, and I come from Maine.
And what's your name, Johnny Reb, and where are you
from?"
"I am Sergeant Richard Kirkland; South Carolina is my
home."

One year later this Southern man would also die,
In the Battle of Chickamauga, where the bullets would fly.
But I hope he's now in heaven, in the army of the Lord,
Because of the tender mercy that he showed in war.

Note: The story is true. There is a monument to Sgt. Richard Kirkland in Fredericksburg, Va, that looks sort of like the Pieta, with a statue of him holding the wounded soldier and giving him water.

***

Lou Roach
Poynette, WI

Today

Rain puddles on the driveway,
absorbing late morning sun.
Each loitering bit of wet
winks as slight breaths of air
riffle the warming water
just enough to tempt winter-locked toes
out of shoes and into April.

Michael Rousseau
NY, NY

Winter Winds

I remember how long it has been
since icy hands gripped my soul, and
the winter of my life settled in.
Vague recollections of a slow black
hearse, a rider-less horse. Harbingers my
life would take a different course.
The church bell tolled to the drummer's
beat. Thousands of mourners lined the
street. The cold and grey, misting rain, mirrored
well a nation's pain.
Then a man shot the man, who shot the man...
I was too young to understand. This all happened
when I was ten and that is when I first felt the
winter settling in.
A switch seemed to flip inside my mind. My thoughts
became as black as blind. Corrupted messages began
to fill my brain. I turned to ways to stop the pain.
It's been forty years since then and the bitter cold
has shown no end. Looking for ways to dull the
rage. Illusionary, temporary stays. Soon I wake
and once again, I face the harsh and driven wind,
of the long cold winter settling in.

Norma J. Crosier
NY, NY

100 Bedford Street

It was June, 1943. We were in the midst of World War II and I had just graduated from Skidmore College. Now what?

I, and several of my classmates, were headed for New York, and some of us had even narrowed our destination down to Greenwich Village where visions of a bohemian life had sparked our imagination. One of my college friends, Nancy, had asked me if I'd like to share an apartment with her as she already had a job waiting for her as an Assistant Buyer at Abraham & Strauss Department Store in Brooklyn.

Something similar was true for me. A representative of American Sugar Refining Company had visited Skidmore in search of "bright young talent," and had offered me a job before I even graduated. This especially pleased my mother who had finally accepted the idea of my living in New York, but needed the added assurance that I actually had a job.

Upon arrival, Nancy and I found temporary lodging at a women's residence, but began looking for our own place right away as we had only a few days before starting our jobs.

We headed for the Village, and the first place the real estate agent showed us was 100 Bedford Street—not a typical apartment building, but surprisingly, a wooden-framed house, just two stories tall.

The owner of the larger building next door, we were told, had been using it as his studio, but recently had refurbished and furnished it as a rental unit.

We couldn't believe our eyes! It had a white picket fence and a gate leading to a small side yard. We entered the house through a Dutch door, took a step down, and were in a compact living room. Two love seats faced each other in front of a fireplace. To the left, beneath the windows, were built-in benches. Just off the living room was a dinette facing the yard. To the right was a den, and tucked under the stairway that led to the second floor, a tiny bathroom. Upstairs were two bedrooms with twin beds in each.

All together, although about the size of a modest one-bedroom apartment with an added second floor, it had all the appearances of a fairy-tale doll house.

The rent was $100 a month, a bit more than we could afford on our starting salaries, but we knew immediately that this was where we wanted to live. Nancy soon discovered that two friends from her hometown in Ellenville, New York, Jean and Pat Taylor, were in the city apartment-hunting, and within two days, four of us had signed a one-year lease and moved in.

I remember that first day vividly. We kept wandering through the house in wonder. "Look at this," Pat remarked. "It has built-in everything—bookcases, storage space, a breakfast nook, and there's a den with a desk, more bookcases and a studio couch in case we have guests. And this fireplace looks like it works!" Meanwhile, I discovered off the living room a narrow, dimly lit, sliver of a room that seemed to come to a point at the end. "Hey, I think this must be the kitchen, but it looks like it hasn't been used much, if at all."

Nancy was rummaging around upstairs and soon hollered down, "These closets are ridiculous—barely room for one or two hangers. Where are we going to put all our clothes?" Jean was busy checking out the bathroom beneath the stairs which, although small, was quite complete with a bathtub, toilet and sink.

Soon we were happily settled in. Living in such limited space would test our skills in getting along, but we managed amazingly well. Pat was two years older than the rest of us. Striking rather than pretty, she held herself a bit aloof with a sophistication that her three roommates were still working on. She had an important job as a doctor's assistant, and soon became active volunteering at one of the local Officers Clubs.

Nancy was an only child and a bit petulant at times, but

could be fun when she wasn't all consumed by her new job. With her round face and short blond hair, she looked much younger than her 21 years.

Jean and I were more alike—carefree and ready for anything that came along. She was, as my mother would say, "as cute as a button" with a ready smile. Her job as a receptionist in a dental office put very few demands on her. As for me, I had an okay face, a pretty good figure, and was blessed with a good disposition and sense of humor.

I remember thinking, *Wow! I'm the luckiest girl in the world. I'm in New York, I have a job, and a wonderful place to live.* I had grown up in a small mill town in Massachusetts and had fond memories of it. Still, it had been my dream from an early age to live in New York City one day. And here I was! I called my family. "You've got to visit soon and see our beautiful new home."

We would soon learn from our landlord that our "new home" was a famous Village landmark, dating back to 1822. I was fascinated, and determined to find out more—what its many uses may have been, and its connection with the larger building next door.

But first things first. Nancy and I were about to join the working world.

As an Assistant Buyer at A & S, she took her new responsibilities very seriously, sometimes waking up at night from a bad dream about it. She brought home all she was learning in the field of fashion, and ways to jazz up our wardrobes.

Mine, working for a sugar company, didn't sound too exciting, but it was on Wall Street, and I soon became intrigued with that part of the city—its history, winding streets, and the "famous" street itself. Once I figured out the subway system, I could get to work in 20 minutes. There must have been a coffee roasting plant nearby because I very distinctly remember coming out of the subway and breathing in that wonderful aroma.

On arrival, I became part of a training group, and after

Norma J. Crosier
NY, NY

several weeks of note-taking about the company, I was assigned to the Statistical Department. It was a small, friendly group and my job involved calculating percentages of various types of sugar being refined and processed.

After a few weeks, however, I began to realize that worrying about pounds of sugar didn't quite fit in with what I had imagined to be a glamorous career, although I wasn't quite sure what that would be. As a Business major, my secretarial skills had been honed to perfection, and it never occurred to me to see if I could transfer to another department. I struggled with my conscience about quitting, after all the effort the firm had made to train and welcome me. In the end, my better judgment told me to stay put for a year. There would be plenty of time to find something more interesting.

Meanwhile, life was proceeding nicely at Bedford Street with the four of us settling into a comfortable routine. It had been a challenge to find room for our clothes in the narrow closets, but the built-in storage space came in handy, and somehow we all managed to leave the house every morning looking quite presentable in our business suits, stockings and high heels, and the white gloves we had to wash out each night.

We spent a lot of our free time that first month sunning in our little yard, keeping our nails in good shape, trying new hair styles, and shopping on our meager salaries for just the right outfit for our Saturday night dates.

I was making some discoveries—our house was originally a one-storied workshop built by the owner next door for his window-making business.

Our kitchen remained pretty much unused, except for a few supplies we kept in the miniature refrigerator for light breakfasts and snacks. We had discovered almost immediately The Blue Mill, a family-owned restaurant nearby. They served wonderful home-style dinners—almost every choice on the menu under $1.00—and we soon became "regulars."

That first summer was unusually hot and we had no air-conditioning—just two or three scattered fans. The two bedrooms upstairs heated up quickly under a hot sun all day. The best relief, we soon found, were the many beaches within easy reach by subway—Reiss Park, the Rockaways and Jones Beach. Best of all was Coney Island which offered not only a sandy beach and cool waves, but much more—the Steeple Chase, Luna Park and Nathan's Hot Dogs!

As happy as we were at that time, the war was never too far from our thoughts. New York was a natural mecca for soldiers and sailors on leave. Grocery items, such as butter, meat and coffee, were rationed, and our favorite cigarettes, Camels, Chesterfields and Lucky Strikes, had been shipped off to servicemen and women. I remember one brand, Sano, which didn't seem to have any tobacco flavor at all, being the only choice at the newsstand.

Later, a second floor was added, some renovations made, and the owner's children used it as their play house.

Each of us had someone special in the service, in my case, Tom Hillgrove, who was with the Air Force building air landing strips in New Guinea. We loved getting those tiny V-mails and were good about writing back, often with a latest photo. Still, caught up in day to day activities, the war could often seem far away.

Weekends were filled with new adventures, all within walking distance. The Village was famous for its exciting night spots, jazz clubs, and outdoor art exhibits in Washington Square. Dates were plentiful with servicemen on leave and through Pat's involvement at the Officers Club. Many Sunday afternoons we headed for Nick's on Greenwich Avenue with our dates to drink beer and enjoy some great jazz—Dizzy Gillespie, Stan Getz, Pee-wee Russell, Gerry Mulligan—in that wonderful, dark, smoke-filled room.

There were loads of parties. Other Skidmore friends had taken apartments in the Village, and one needed very little excuse to get together on a Saturday evening. We especially loved showing off our little home.

It's quite famous—the owner told us it's designated as the smallest complete house in Manhattan.

We were becoming quite sophisticated New Yorkers, we thought, and I remember one way we tried to enhance our image was to memorize the list of bestselling books in the *New York Times Book Review* so that we could casually work their names into our conversation at parties. We didn't actually read the books, but were able to rattle off titles with great ease.

One weekend I'm sure we'd never forget. Pat had offered to take care of her boss' highly-valued miniature Schnauzer while he was away for the weekend, and we felt very special taking it for walks around the neighborhood. On Saturday, it somehow escaped from our yard and disappeared. We were frantic. How would we ever find that little dog in this huge city? We searched everywhere in the area, asked everyone in sight if they had seen it, and put up "Lost" notices at various spots offering a reward. Pat hardly dared to think what she would tell her boss on Monday. We had no news for the next agonizing twenty-four hours; then finally on Sunday afternoon, an elderly man appeared with our little charge in tow. Fortunately, he turned down our reward, which would have been quite modest anyway, but we insisted he come in for a "thank you" drink.

Once summer ended, we learned how wonderful New York weather could be in late September and October; then, with the first chill in the air, we started to enjoy our fireplace and entertaining at home.

It was even a tea room for a while. I visualized two or three small tables and chairs in the living room, and guests enjoying their tea and cakes.

One day I announced, "Hey, how about having dinner here tonight? I'll get a nice steak and some baking potatoes, and we'll put our kitchen to use." I was by no means a great cook, but I knew enough to put together something fairly

Norma J. Crosier
NY, NY

basic. With its dim lighting, it was hard to tell what condition the stove was in, and it didn't occur to me that it might need cleaning.

That evening, I turned on the oven and very quickly some accumulated grease caught fire, and four hysterical women were running around trying to decide what to do. Finally one of us called the Fire Department, and soon four firemen appeared at our door with ladders, hatchets and miles of hose. They trooped in, found the kitchen, and quickly put out the flames. One of them even took a few extra minutes to scrape off all the old grease and relight the oven to be sure of no recurrence. The potatoes then went in as planned.

We were so relieved we invited them to stay and have a beer with us. They declined the beer, but indeed did stay for a short while, and we had a great time sharing stories about our adventures in the city and their exciting lives as firemen.

"How did you girls find this place?" they wanted to know. "We've passed it many times, but we didn't know anyone lived here."

It's a very old building, a landmark, and has had a variety of uses. Just before we moved in, it was the owner's art studio.

We were equally curious about them. "Did you always know that you wanted to be firemen?" we asked. "Do you live at the firehouse all the time, or do you have homes and families elsewhere in the city?" Soon though, they said they'd have to get back. "But we're in the neighborhood so I'm sure we'll see you all again. And just give us a call if you have any more trouble with that stove." We thanked them and they were gone with all their gear as quickly as they had arrived.

When I learned that my mother and dad were coming for a visit, we did an extra good cleaning job. We always tidied up Saturday mornings, but this time, with our first parental-type visit, we actually moved furniture while vacuuming rather than just vacuuming around things. This was our introduction to those large, ugly water bugs known to many

New Yorkers. They didn't like being disturbed, but were too fast to catch and scuttled back to where they came from until the next big cleaning.

When my folks arrived, things were looking pretty ship-shape. Mother remarked, "My goodness, what a charming place. And I must say I'm impressed that the four of you manage so well in such a small space." Dad was fascinated too and spent a lot of time examining the building from the outside.

Can you imagine, Dad? This little house is over 100 years old and in such good, solid condition. People walking by are always surprised when they see it.

The subject of the rarely-used kitchen never came up, fortunately, as we hurried our guests over to the Blue Mill for dinner.

Strangely enough, I don't remember any serious arguments about chores and household bills. Naturally, there were bound to be some minor squabbles, such as, "Are you going to take all evening in the tub?" or "Who took my stockings that were hanging in the bathroom?" And between Jean and Pat, "Excuse me, but isn't that my red sweater you're wearing?" I think the closest we came to a fight was one evening when Pat decided I was being a little too friendly with her date. Later, when our guests had left, she accosted me with, "Of all the unmitigated nerve!" or calling me an "unmitigated" something. Either way, I had to look it up the next day!

In the spring, we were thrilled to discover that our house had become one of the stops on tours of the Village. Often, we would hang out the upstairs windows and greet the group gathered in front, telling them how much we loved living there. On one occasion, at least, we went a step further, "Come on in. Let us show you around."

As June approached, we began to think about renewing our lease. However, Jean and Pat learned that their mother had just relocated into the city and decided they could save some money if they lived with her. Sadly, Nancy and I made plans to move to an apartment on nearby Perry Street, one that we could afford by ourselves.

That last afternoon, after the final carton had been taped and suitcase snapped shut, we sat glumly looking around, feeling close to tears. It struck each of us that we were going to miss our lives together in this amazing little house more than we had ever imagined. Jean was the first to break the silence.

"Come on! Let's cheer ourselves up and invite some of our neighbors over for a farewell party."—And that's how we said goodbye to a very special place and time in our lives.

Now, many years later, I still have more sleuthing to do. The present owner tells me that for the past fifteen years, he's used 100 Bedford Street solely as his guesthouse. But I'd love to be able to share stories with all the others who may have lived there and loved it as much as we did while it was still a rental unit.

Anne Hammond
Woolwich, ME

Brookings Bay

At high tide when the Bay seems to be fixed—
A broad, bountiful plate of silver and blue,
Sparkling ripples, surging white caps, flashing with fish—
The water begins to withdraw.

At low tide when water seems to have departed forever—
Bottomland flats are a restful gray,
Wormers scrape the layers of silt,
Birds feed along the rivulets—
The water begins to return.

The Bay is the body of water that doesn't exist,
The body of air that's always getting lost.

***

First Snow

With great, soft flakes, the vestibule of winter
Arrives, drawing dark silhouette of deer
Across the meadow. Ice sheets splinter
Underfoot; ears shift to locate fear.
A flock of ducks flies in from the south
Attracting the attention of owls and hawks
Who know speed and stealth will fill every mouth.
Marsh hawk swoops above the cord grass stalks
Eyeing the flock. Planning his feast of one
He sorties swiftly from oak to pine limb.
Angling with ease under clouded sun,
He makes pass after pass, adjusting only tail trim.
He waits for a duck to carelessly stray;
The bird he will pluck from the winter's gray.

Marilyn E. Canavan
Waterville, ME

Progress

The oak across the way
is far too assertive;
each year it assumes more
of the horizon.
In the summer, my neighbor's cape
shrinks beneath its mass,
and in autumn it flings acorns everywhere.
What's worse, in winter, it has no shame
stripping outright to flaunt
its gnarled nakedness.
There will be no end to its bold airs
spreading everywhere
if we do not soon teach it who really holds sway.
After all, it can be replaced
with asphalt.

Byron von Rosenberg
House Springs, MO

Advice from My Aunt Winnie

In honor and memory of Winifred Taylor Laubach

The advice from my Aunt Winnie
When my ears were turning red
Was clear, concise and firm,
"Put that cap back on your head!"
But it wasn't only practical.
She was kind and wise
And the words she said could often
Take you by surprise.
There was the time I lost
My very favorite toy
And she knew just what to say
To help that little boy.
"I've looked everywhere," I said,
"That it could ever be!"
"Then look somewhere it couldn't!"
And her words helped me to see
Not only just the toy I found
But other things as well,
Ideas, dreams and meaning
In the stories I now tell.
"Dare to think and dare to dream
And seek out your own way!"
Advice from my Aunt Winnie
I've followed to this day.

Bill Tucker
Aurora, OH

An Old Man's Reflections

Excerpts from the memoir "Sing for Me, Betty Lee"

It seems that a certain rhythm of calmness overcomes the crew of a ship when there are long uninterrupted days of sailing on the way home. In the Pacific waters, off the coast of southern California and Central America, when the nights were lighted by a moon that went from gibbous to full to the days of wane, the crew would climb upon the deck-loaded timber and sing sad songs. Either a battery-powered radio or one with a long extension cord would pick up the music from some high-powered station. Songs like *I'll Be Seeing You* and *As Time Goes By* and *Sentimental Journey* would tighten our throats, and the yearning for home was so palpable that it was difficult to talk, or even look at someone whose eyes may have become bright with some lonely memory.

In all the time I would spend at sea, the romance of those nights would never be repeated. There was something about the silver glow of the moonstream, that stretched from the St. Augustine to the blackness of the nighttime horizon, that encouraged the dolphin to play in it. It seemed that hundreds would simultaneously break the water in their parabolic dives, and either tirelessly repeat them or be replaced by others. If the moonstream coincided with the ship's wake, the hundreds would multiply into thousands, and we would watch until we tired of the show and returned to our own sentimental maunderings.

Betty Lee's face was in my mind's eye, superimposed on the back of my eyelids and on the face of the moon.

There are observations about the war I will make here that were formulated, for the most part, long after the present chronology of this story. In Tom Brokaw's book *The Greatest Generation,* he repeats over and over again that the

Bill Tucker
Aurora, OH

Second World War was the defining experience in the lives of just about everyone who was in the service. This was certainly true in my case, not because of anything heroic I did—I, like the vast majority of people in uniform, never heard a shot fired in anger—but because it gave me the experience of not being at home when I grew up. Country boys and small-town boys and city boys and boys from the country's ghettos had a chance to grow up somewhere else. And, in some sort of national epiphany, it transformed the culture of the nation.

It is difficult to see any benefit in that bloody, maiming war. For many of those who survived it, there was a tendency to subtract the years they spent in the service from their lives, to grieve over what was lost. In my case it was a magnificent addition, more than my life would have been without it. And I think that is true, but unrealized, of the lives of those who think of it only in negative terms.

I believe that everyone who sees a war sees a different one. Mine was simple, unthreatening. But I also believe that everyone who came back wanted something different from what he wanted when he went in. Some of us wanted more, some wanted less. Some of the others didn't want anything. There was just nothing left in them. It was all gone, left on some island in the Pacific or in some field in Europe. As I said, I was one of the lucky ones who, by luck and circumstance, just brushed up against the war as it was leaving.

Bonnie Hatchett
Little Rock, AR

Charlie Red/The Gift

When we love someone we look at that person with eyes of innocence and, what we behold is the unblemished soul. That love frees the beloved to remove the mask and thus allows the liberty to stand naked for scrutiny. Any imperfections are viewed through eyes of love. Recently I saw my father in a dream, although he has been dead for over thirty years. In the dream he came to the campus of the university where I teach. He was wearing a mask and I stated, "It's okay, Dad, you can take off the mask, I know that it is you and I am not afraid. I know that you are dead." That reluctance is illustrative of the love that he had for his children, not wanting to cause any discomfort, yet wanting to make his presence known. He often said that his children were his heart. As the mask was removed I was able to gaze into his eyes and to see the pureness of his soul. I have written poems about my father, read them and shared them with others to validate his existence and the impact that he had on the lives of many others, as well as the impact and sustaining power of a father's love.

People often view things, objects and people differently because that view again is related to the viewer's perspective. I can recall, many years ago, at age twelve, I had an interesting revelation or as some would say an epiphany. As I looked at my father, I realized that there were those who would find him unattractive. I marveled at the fact that I had never "seen" this before. Weighing well over 250 pounds, with an ethnic mix (Creole, Irish and Native American) that exhibited itself in red ruddy skin, red curly hair and freckles over every exposed part of his body. Although I had seen him everyday of my life, I had not really seen the freckles or felt that, "Charlie Red," as he was called, stood out in the African American or as we were called in those days the "colored"

Bonnie Hatchett
Little Rock, AR

community.

I suddenly realized and was able to really reflect on a passage in the Bible that states, "love covers a multitude of sins." Love is such a powerful, powerful emotion. Love can blind us to the ugliness of reality and in so doing the stressors of life. It can give us the support that is needed when we encounter difficulties. It can also allow us to have compassion and acceptance for those different from ourselves. When I reflect on the character of my father, I realize that those realizations were great gifts, that have transcended time and that have enriched my life.

The poems and essays that I write about my father, and the reading and sharing of them validates his existence and allows me to share that special connection with others. I love to write about my reaction to relationships with significant others in my life, some nurturing, some devaluing and some supportive. Such writing is a validation of the importance of support, yet not a vendetta or blaming against those who have caused pain. Those who cause pain are in a state of unresolved grief themselves. The process of healing, of reclaiming ones self brings about the realization of this.

Diana Woodcock
Midlothian, VA

Tamed by the Desert

The psalmist advises
be still and wait patiently.*
Simone Weil noted one obtains
the most precious gifts

not by searching but by
waiting for them. So here
I am, still and waiting—
listening for elaborate echoes,

levels and opposites,
the ubiquitous turn.
August, desert steaming,
gleaming in relentless sun.

Sitting among oryxes and shy
gazelle, I write love letters to
spoonbills and alligators back
in the Everglades, recalling rain—

drenched days among them.
Whirling with burning coals in
my hands, I feel no pain. A white
cat's become my guardian.

Bones aching in stillness now,
the desert having tamed me,
I meditate, prostrate myself on a
sandstone jebel-flat-top hillock

Diana Woodcock
Midlothian, VA

of Ras Abrouk, and I wait
for the sea to reach me,
the shamal to rustle the wings
of the white-throated robin.

*Psalms 37:7a

***

Robert Erickson
Round Pond, ME

Winds of Change

The technical winds of change are blowing
I can see it happening every day
Little hand-held boxes with screens aglowing
Thumbs poking in an unusual way.

I truly don't know what to make of it
The electronic world setting the pace
Cell phones are the worst, giving me a fit
I prefer talking to a real live face

No use in my complaining though
I'm just to old for it I guess
I'll feel the wind wherever I go
But rest assured I'll have my GPS

James McKenna
Hallowell, ME

Buying Coffee from the Happy Youth of Mao Zedong

Pretty in their red shirts
and loose tan pants, they
seem like cheerful comrades,
like Mao's happy youth,
gladly pushing forward
History's heavy wheel.
And her particularly,
as she leans forward
her pale blue bra strap
for a moment revealed.
She seems serene in beauty's dialectic,
no fear of Fate's many tricks,
no fear of next year's wants,
as she sweetly asks, "Senior Discount?"

***

Patrick T. Randolph
Murphysboro, IL

Mountain Path

Raven bathes in snow—
Black eyes flickering with light,
Reflecting small flakes;

The universe seems to stop—
Raven prints left on the ground.

e. w. oestreich
Damariscotta, ME

In Quiet Words

In quiet words to yield the brambled
field

        and set adrift so near to
        journey's

end an evensong is legacy enough.
Set no small stone.
If one would come to understand the
land I've traveled through

        just listen to the quiet
        words

the edging sea allows; the sift a Winter's night
might pray with flakes of snow. In these
you'll breathe, in these you'll hear
a voice
and realize we've met before.

Kathy McHugh
Dover, NH

Stuck in the Parking Lot of My Old Junior High

I never figured I'd be stuck here like this. I was in the library for less than an hour; just needed a quiet place to complete my income tax forms then read a magazine or two. When I came back out I unlocked the front door of my car, but the automatic lock switch for the other doors did not work. I got in and tried to start my car, but it stalled, even in neutral. So I ended up calling roadside assistance and was told that help would arrive in forty-five minutes, which grew into an hour and a half, then two hours.

So here I am, stuck in the community center parking lot better known to me as the playground of my old junior high, back in the early 1970's. I have plenty to read, plenty to write. But I suddenly got caught up in a vivid memory of the unathletic me swinging at a ball tied to a tetherball pole, cheered on against my opponent jumping to hit the ball in the opposite direction. Then I look toward the outskirts of the pavement remembering me in my one piece green gym suit which I felt like I had already outgrown, warning the gym teacher that I should not be an outfielder as I'm no good at throwing anything long distances, to which she shouted, "I don't care! Get out there! Throw it! Throw the ball!" So I gave it my all and the ball travelled like a magnet to hit my friend Shannon in the side of the face. The next thing I remember after going to the nurse's office was that her mouth was wired shut, due to her broken jaw.

Our playground was also the setting for another form of recreation—the card game "Knuckles." I don't remember exactly how it was played, but I do remember that if you lost, the winner held the cards sideways and fanned, elevated them just above the fisted hands, then came down hard on the loser's knuckles, turning them bright red and bloody, especially if it was someone they hated. No one ever hurt me, but I witnessed a lot of brutal revenge. I also remember sitting on the edge of the playground not being able to get up when the bell rang, as I had sat on gum.

You might think that being inside the school was safer, but it wasn't. When I enter my old school through the door closest to the street and walk up the now green vinyl covered stairs, I look to my right, where Miss C.'s seventh grade English class was. I still remember several students in front of me knocking on the glass window of that door jokingly letting Miss C. know that she was holding class too long. She responded by opening the door and slapping across all of the faces in front of her, then haunting us with Edgar Allen Poe and Alfred Hitchcock films for the rest of the week. Nearby are the stairs I fell down, distracted while humming the theme song to the television show "Room 222," my only exposure to life beyond grammar school.

Around the corner is the classroom where we were forced to dissect frogs. Also the intimidating Mr. H.'s math class where he made a girl cry, defending his actions with the statement, "You can dish it out, but you can't take it in." The fact that Mr. H. ended up marrying Miss C. was hard to register. What a household that must have been, we thought. Upstairs to the left was Mrs. K.'s eighth grade English class; the one who threatened, "If you do that again I'm going to splat it right in your face!" Then I realized she was talking to me, the one mastering the bubble gum.

I can't say that all of my experiences were bad ones; it's just that the good times were few and far between. My poetry was often featured in the school newspaper and literary magazine. I received an award for perfect attendance for the entire two years I was there. I enjoyed and learned a lot from the Dickens-intensive reading assignments of Mrs. A., my seventh grade English teacher. I learned to cook and sew in home economics, even though I ran over my finger with the sewing machine. My friend Kate and I produced and performed a campaign song radio show about the 1972 presidential candidates. And the icing on the cake was our eighth grade graduation trip to Weirs Beach, the arcades and a Mount Washington boat cruise on Lake Winnipesaukee.

Okay—back to the bad stuff. There seemed to be a conflict between our open campus privileges and corporal punishment—like getting the strap in the office if one like my brother was thought to be in need of further discipline. He was also rushed to the hospital with severe abdominal pain and was set to have his appendix out until he told the doctor that the last thing he ate was twelve jelly donuts. Speaking of poor nutrition, I had multiple appointments with a dermatologist who provided ultraviolet light treatments for my acne while I maintained my regular diet of greasy hotdogs and donuts. One day my friends and I were running back to school from the donut shop, and looked back to find our suddenly missing friend Nancy had slammed into a parking meter and passed out on the ground. A student in my science class was out of school for two months due to her overdosing on heroin.

It all happened here because of this building, back when everyone was friendly and full of purpose before we moved on to the new Dover High, where the social seemed to outshine and outweigh the academic. But I have so many memories of my time here—both then and now. When I hear of communities disgusted with old schools and cajoling city councils to fund brand new school buildings, I wish they could see what has been done to preserve my old junior high.

The tow truck has arrived. The playground is quiet now, and the Green Bean Café operates at the former cafeteria, creating healthy soups and sandwiches rather than greasy fries and hot dogs. Soda has been replaced with healthy juice and water. The Senior Center and Family Services have taken over the back of the building. The superintendent of schools and Dover Adult Learning Center occupy the front half.

Kathy McHugh
Dover, NH

I feel fortunate to be able to return to this building that was my old junior high and this playground turned parking lot. Still, no matter how many times I've been here, I feel that I always come out better than the person I was when I went in....

***

Catherine Wang Hsu
Malden, MA

Flight

I left myself behind
got into the speedy train.

On and on,
it went so fast.

A thousand miles
flew quickly by.

The fuel gave out;
the train stopped.

It left me there to
find myself.

DiTa Ondek
Friendship, ME

And We Came to Grief

a perfect storm challenges
the heartiest of sailors
circumnavigators who spin
the big blue watery marble
that engages the boy in every seafarer
wave, wind, gale and gust
convulsing
the 55 foot ketch on a port tack
keel over, capsizing the best of swabbies
who sang such tales and chanteys of
of the Black Ballers and sailors grog
brave men upset by the squall
left behind in watery
graveyards—by sage and sea.

***

Byron Hoot
Wexford, PA

Sunlight

The sun at evening
Does not blind me.
I look directly into
It—no squinting
Just looking into
The face of someone
You've known for a long time.

Beth Ellen Jack
Huntington Beach, CA

Like Ophelia

For my daughter in the hospital

You came and went like a phantom image,
complexion pallid, more translucent than
waxy gardenias, petals spent and bruised.
You drift as greedy waters confiscated
what was left of you. How your wrists dangle
like broken stems, to fulfill a dire horoscope
most of us ignore, until we sense new perils—
blurs our vision. Even in California,
landscape once bright as tinfoil, can fold over,
as if the coppice outside bleeds, trees shake
like green petticoats, people bend like praying mantis
in the distance, dodging pellets of rain.

I no longer recognize patterns or designs;
what was familiar tilts like a fun-house mirror,
words make caterwauls, as if consonants and vowels
no longer exist. Still later, your hands remain folded
like Ophelia's before someone arranges them,
almost like a benediction when the heroine sleeps,
until I bend over with a kiss.

Naya Clifford
Waldo County, ME

The Bear

Like an old well-loved aunt, the June morning wrapped her hot sweaty arms around Crocker's burly shoulders. Sitting on the small screened porch, Steve cracked open a can of beer while Crocker enjoyed a hearty breakfast of red hot dogs. He swallowed, eyes narrowing at his friend over the rim of the can. Steve never understood Crocker's affection for those *things*. They sported red casings the color of an old neon beer sign and a similar flavor in Steve's opinion. Smacking his lips happily, Crocker smiled at his friend's disgust. He belched for emphasis and reached down to grab another can of beer from the well worn Coleman cooler. As he snapped the metal lid shut, he saw a thin, scraggly man come loping into his yard. The guy's eyes darted wildly behind him as he ran towards Crocker's door.

Crocker recognized the man as Paul Smith, or Smitty; folks in town said he had a camp over across the road, set back into the woods. Crocker thought maybe he had a dope patch as there was no cabin, nor shack nor tent of any kind over there that could be seen. Uncertain of his neighbor's intentions, Crocker rose from his chair and grabbed his shotgun, from where it rested right next to the screen door.

Slowly and with some measured style, he raised the shot gun level to Smitty's approaching forehead. Crocker clicked the gun's chamber purposefully as his fiery green eyes took a bead over the barrel.

"Hi there, neighbor." Crocker had said evenly, as he rocked the shotgun back and forth. Smitty's rabbit like glance followed the barrel, then darted back over his shoulder for what ever he thought might be chasing him.

"You in some kind of trouble?"

Smitty's mouth pulled in a tight crease, forehead sweaty under his dirty Boston Red Sox baseball cap. The black flies swarmed his ears.

"Two black bears just fell into my house and are eating all of my food!"

Crocker raised his grey eye brows, and turned to Steve,

"So buddy you said you've never hunted bear? Want to?"

Smiling broadly, Steve nodded his head and grinned. Steve had hunted deer as a young man with Crocker after the war, but since he had developed Lou Gehrig's he hadn't been able to get into the woods. His legs and arms just wouldn't listen to his commands any more.

Hopping from foot to foot, Smitty looked frantic, he pleaded, "Well, can you come over and help? I don't have a gun."

Crocker chortled in disbelief. Everyone owned a gun here, well most people in fact owned several guns. He decided that Smitty must be a dope growing granola type from Massachusetts, lost in the north woods!

"Damned hippies," he said under his breath as he turned and said, "Steve, you comin'?"

"Hell yeah!" he said getting up on his crutches.

Crocker carried his shotgun and grabbed a rifle from the corner of the porch for Steve. They hurriedly shuffled across the little front yard over to Crocker's red pick up truck. Steve tossed his crutches hastily into the bed of the truck as the three of them slid into the cab. Smitty's bony finger pointed to the woods road across the street.

Ferns grew tall and the hazy daylight spun lazily through the dense tree limbs. Crocker had barely pulled into the dense thicket of spruce trees when his neighbor started motioning for him to stop. Crocker couldn't see anything that resembled a house, much less a house with a caved in roof which two bears had fallen into.

"It's right here." Smitty grunted impatiently still waving his pointing finger.

Smitty gestured to a little path on the left, and said, "It's up that path about a hundred yards."

Crocker knew Steve couldn't walk that uneven ground

with the way his legs had been working, so he parked the pickup truck on the woods road where Steve could sit with the rifle.

"Steve you stay here and I'll try and see if I can flush them towards you."

Hurrying up the worn path across roots and a thick bed of soft rust colored needles, Crocker asked, "Where is your house?"

They came up a small rise in the path with nothing in sight. Smitty stopped, cocked his pony tailed head and rolled his eyes.

"It's right there." He pointed to what looked like a bear's den.

Crocker thought he was kidding or on drugs. He had heard of kids like this doing strange things. He looked at the twenty something kid in the baseball hat, his flannel shirt bought from the LL Bean store in Freeport, no doubt. The kid looked like he wanted to be a "woodsman" and had bought all the right clothes out of the pictures in a catalogue. Although covered in some dirt and debris, his clothes themselves had been washed recently and bore no chain grease stains of a real working woodsman.

"Oh come on man, are you messing with me?" The disbelief lay bare in Crocker's tone.

He followed the hippie kid up the low brush covered rise as the remains of an underground shelter, with the ceiling caved in, opened before them. He could see that the tunnel Smitty had pointed out was indeed the only "door." Apparently, Smitty had really gotten into the "back to the land" idea and had built his own earth berm cave house.

Clearly, he had not anticipated the weight of other creatures who might walk on top of his "home." From the shredded green plastic and chewed food containers below it appeared as if a bear had fallen through his tarp covered roof and enjoyed a picnic.

Naya Clifford
Waldo County, ME

Crocker swiveled his head looking around for a bear. He heard the distinctive snap of jaws come from behind the spruce grove down the hill a few yards to his left. Peering into the dark green boughs, he spotted a large female black bear, in a bad mood. The mother glared at him and shook her head to keep away the flies. She snapped her powerful jaws together and grunted to intimidate the men. When that didn't work she thumped her front paws on the ground and clicked her teeth. Crocker had seen this same sow bear and her cub earlier that spring meandering casually through his front yard. This particularly large female bear had become a local legend. Every hunter from Sherman Mills to Smyrna had taken a shot at her, and one old guide claimed he had clipped her ear. Today, Crocker was again close enough to see her notched ear as she bellowed unhappily at him.

He lifted his gun and shot near her feet, kicking up some needles and forest debris. He missed intentionally. He respected this bear. At her age, this was probably her last cub, and he felt if she had earned her place in the woods.

Unfortunately, his shot only irritated her. She grunted, shook her mammoth head back and forth and clicked her teeth together more furiously. She made thunderous angry noises calling for her baby.

Crocker felt he had to flush the cub if they were all going to avoid a nasty fight. He drew in a breath and ignoring his better instincts he walked intently towards the entry way, pointing his gun. He shouted out into the darkness.

"Hey little bear!"

As his eyes adjusted to the dimness, his heart beat like the helicopters he and Steve used to ride on. He felt the old intense rush, the metal tingle in his mouth of fear mixed with excitement as he crawled into the hovel's front entry.

Then he heard the "woodsman" cry fearfully out from above.

"The cub is up here! He and the mother bear just took off towards your buddy." Crocker quickly shimmied out of the entrance, stood and squeezed off another round into the air to give Steve a heads up.

Hearing the shots, he leaned against the truck in his worn blue jeans. Steve grew angry with himself for not being there. The heavy gun powder scent hung desperately in the humid air. His frustration surged, he had always been part of the action and now here he was, trapped by his own body. He cursed and spat. He had been coming up to see Crocker for better than ten years, since they were 20 year old privates together in another life, jumping helicopters and fighting side by side in terrain far more rugged than this old woods path.

Yet, despite all of his trips to the north woods, Steve had never seen a black bear. He had always felt kindred with the black bears. He went into his own "cave state of mind" each winter and emerged, hesitantly into mud season each spring. He wondered if he would even come out of his cave next year, or even if there would be another full winter.

A soft, thumping scuffle sound broke through his reflections, and he glanced up toward the path. He exhaled softly as the huge sow black bear ran at him full speed. He drew in a sharp breath, his muscles tightening, his hands unconsciously gripped his crutches. He didn't have time to pick up the gun.

"Well, if I'm going to die, this sure beats the damned disease," he mused.

The bear ran at him with her mouth open, spittle flapping as she panted. Steve watched her with awe.

The mother bear looked back over her shoulder and so did Steve, and he saw the over 100 pound cub following as fast as he could. The mother bear ran past Steve, scuffing up dirt as she turned in front of the truck. She treated Steve like any other tree in the forest, an object to be gone around. The baby ran by just the same and in a flash they were crashing into the brush and out of sight.

Steve hobbled over to where the bears had entered into

Naya Clifford
Waldo County, ME

the thicket. He noticed a piece of coarse black fur clinging to a bramble. Trembling slightly, he reached out and picked it up. Raising the fur to his nose, he inhaled deeply. He smelled adrenaline and bear grease mixed with pine and fur. Not pleasant, but all bear. He smiled as he put the fur into his shirt pocket. Real bear medicine, for dreaming through the winter. Hearing more footsteps, he craned his neck around to see Crocker and Smitty running his way.

Crocker grinned yelling, "So you got to see your bear!"

"I got to see both of them, so close I could almost touch them. They sure smelled strong." Steve glowed, his eyes twinkling, grinning ear to ear like a dog after a good game of Frisbee.

Crocker laughed, he knew bears smelled awful, strong was a compliment. He turned to his neighbor, "Nice place you built there kid!" he chortled.

Smitty looked at the ground, like a shamed boy and shrugged as he said, "Well at least they didn't eat everything."

Steve looked at them questioningly.

Crocker tilted his stubble covered chin slyly and said, "Looks like they ripped open the cooler and searched through it, cracked all the cans of beer. They ate everything they thought smelled like food. Tooth paste included."

"Well, almost everything." Smitty said, as he held up an untouched package.

Crocker smiled, and caught his friends eyes, as he admitted, "Yeah, even the bears know better than to eat those damned red hot dogs."

Sally Belenardo
Branford, CT

The Smell of Soil

His shovel makes room in the ground
for roots of azalea and quince. He inhales
the scent of the planet's skin to viscera, to soul.
What does it smell like?
Like nothing else, composed of everything:

Crumbled bedrock, mountain worn to sand,
enriched with all that ever lived
and left their flesh and feathers, leaves and flowers
to the world.

Loam piles up around the holes he digs
in the ubiquitous grave filled with life.
Clods tumble, break; earthworms wriggle.
Grubs curl in circles. Ants hoist white eggs away.

He ponders mysteries buried here,
where those who die will disappear,
where filth is purified and putrefaction
blends with rain, becomes perfume
distilled in cask of earth,

reminiscent of something beyond memory,
primordial, elemental,
seeping into the veins
of every leaf in his gardens.

George Wentz
Sturgeon Bay, WI

March

It's a joyless time,
—March,
the senses deprived
of Nature's gifts.

Even the sound of it,
—March,
is dead, unlike
May, June, July.

Sparkling snowflakes
put on a festive face
for Christmas,
but now

snow is a dirty word.
—March,
trees still asleep,
creeks frozen.

If only the chirp
of one bird could be heard,
I would know
I have not gone deaf.

Just one green leaf,
just one small bud,
I would know
of winter's end.

George Wentz
Sturgeon Bay, WI

No, the icy wind
still bites my face.
—March,
it makes me wait,
and want, and wait...

***

P. C. Moorehead
North Lake, WI

Rooted

I am rooted in the earth.
I stand here tall,
my trunk straight,
my bark rough,
my leaves beginning to bud.

I am who I am:
tall,
straight,
rough,
budding,
rooted

in love.

Tom Crowley
Lincolnville, ME

Snow Carvings

I thought we would miss winter this year.

There was no snow in November
And I was sorry I hauled the boat.
There was no snow in December
And I was sorry Christmas wasn't white.

In January, we froze and pipes burst
But it still didn't snow.
In February, the winds came
And they brought the snow.

Dusting to powder to inches to feet,
Drifts covered the dinghy.
The snow was so deep that it slid
Off the roof of the woodshed

Onto the stone patio
Where the winds carved words
I did not understand
But tried to read before the winds
Changed them, or me.

I thought we would miss winter this year
But now I know that I would really
Miss winter if winter missed me.

Louis Arthur Norton
West Simsbury, CT

Desolation Shoal

At Maine's Snow Harbor, the rising sun dimly lit the bedroom of a lobsterman who embraced his wife and left their bed. It was mid-winter. She did not want him to go, but she said nothing. When his warm bare feet touched the cold floor and the chilly air struck his nude flesh, the lobsterman who usually delighted in the harshness of winter, had second thoughts about going out. Still, he had promised to take his son out on his new lobster boat and help pull traps off Desolation Shoal in the morning. Desolation Shoal, an island a half-mile off the Maine coast, was a craggy granite rock adorned with a ruffled skirt of shiny brown kelp that disappears twice a day under the high tide to form a breaker-roll blemish on the sea. It was one of many shoals whose geology was relentlessly sculptured by the North Atlantic Ocean—and an ideal place for lobsters to breed and feed.

Snow Harbor men either harvested lobsters from the seafloor near the rocky Maine coastal shore or had jobs that supported the cottage industry of lobstering in some way. The lobstermen labored atop ocean swells in a twenty-five to forty-foot single engine vessel that had a small forward cabin and a fairly large open-deck-cockpit aft.

Ed Merrell, the lobsterman, was a tall rugged man with a shock of thick red hair and a weather-tanned complexion that contrasted with his deep blue eyes. He exuded a self-confidence that had been honed from experience working at his demanding and dangerous job. A taciturn man, when he did speak, he spoke quietly and deliberately. He loved his wife Kate and particularly his thirteen-year old son Billy. Ed looked forward to taking the boy winter lobstering on his new boat called the *Katie M* named after his wife. This would be a chance for them to further their bond and for to Ed to teach Billy some cold weather lobster fishing skills.

Louis Arthur Norton
West Simsbury, CT

Billy, not a child and not quite a man, had red hair and dark brown eyes like his father and intended to become a lobsterman someday. The boy was eager to join his dad—but he was apprehensive. Billy could not swim and often got seasick. Ed, however, was a strong swimmer and rough weather never bothered him. He was confident that any son of his would overcome these small problems.

His legs firmly planted, Ed raised his arms and stretched as high as he could in his bedroom while listening to the wind in the nearby pines. It sounded like an easterly breeze. These were ideal conditions. Ed quickly dressed in the cold and dark, and then woke Billy who tumbled out of bed. The boy groped for his shirt, trousers and the thick red woolen socks his mother had lovingly knitted for him. Billy's thoughts were still fogged by sleep, yet he became increasingly excited as he thought about the lobstering trip with his father.

Ed's wife, Kate, heard Billy dressing. He was noisier than usual, fumbling about his room and humming a sea chantey that he learned from his dad—probably in anticipation of the day ahead. Kate pulled the covers up to her chin deciding to take advantage of rare opportunity to loiter in bed. Meanwhile Ed got down to the serious business of cooking a hearty Maine breakfast of fishcakes, re-warmed baked beans, and porridge with maple syrup washed down with piping-hot coffee. They would be well nourished for their day at sea.

Maine's winter weather could be treacherous and, in case there was trouble, there were few others out on the water. Ed's years of experience caused him to be cautious, but not fearful. He considered fear as more of a woman's concern and he was too much of a man to display it. In fact, when Ed and Kate were first married they argued about whether he should put up his lobster boat until spring, but the price of winter lobster was profitable even though the frequent storms took a toll on his gear.

Louis Arthur Norton
West Simsbury, CT

Ed worked hard and made a comfortable living for the family. Over their fifteen years of marriage Kate had learned to accept Ed's ways taking comfort in his work ethic and competence. There were occasional expressions of love, but mostly their marriage provided companionship and a son whom they both cherished. Kate's long straight prematurely gray hair made her appear older than she was and her blue-gray eyes looked sad to many. Both features may have been attributed to her frequent dreams—actually terrible nightmares; the dread of the loneliness from losing her husband at sea and having to raise Billy without his father. And if Billy became a lobsterman, she might lose him too. She did not discuss these dreams with anybody, especially Ed.

The backdoor slammed as her husband, son and their chocolate Labrador retriever, Umber, went out into the yard. Kate thought anyone electing to go lobstering on such a cold morning had to be mad. They would probably not think about her until they returned with their catch and had the lobsters safely put into holding tanks. Dry snow grinding beneath two pairs of boots made a distinct sound that traveled through her partly opened bedroom window. Ed's sharp commands to Billy to "Untie the lines and get onboard" were punctuated by barks from the dog, the animal emphasizing his master's exhortations.

The early morning sun lit two large boulders angled toward each other as though in conversation. They marked the narrow path that led to the water's edge outlined in frozen salt-suds. Because it was January, there was some ice around the lobster boat that would take them to the waters off Desolation Shoal. The lobsterman maintained his motors taking pride in their condition. The motor coughed once, sputtered, then with a snarl abruptly burst into life with a reassuring roar. The sound of the *Katie M.'s* engine ripped the early morning silence asunder and a black cloud of exhaust lazily rose into the frosty air. Billy went forward to cast the mooring line loose. Inside the house Kate closed her

Louis Arthur Norton
West Simsbury, CT

eyes as the drone from the motor's exhaust deepened, then gradually the steady sound faded into the distance.

Ed steered to port, quickly glanced at his compass then headed northeast by east toward the bay's mouth and the open ocean. A foghorn mournfully moaned in the distance announcing the arrival of a chowder-like frost-mist that quickly moved in from the east. There was just enough visibility to navigate to the Puffin Point headland through the crooked channel that cut between the many small islands. The lobsterman had motored through this nasty stretch of water in fog and darkness many times; his skill was such that he could find his way anywhere in the bay blindfolded. From the mouth of the channel Ed planned to take a northeasterly course straight for Desolation Shoal. The low tide would expose the seaweed-covered ledge. It was a cold morning and the *Katie M.* was farther out than most lobstermen cared to venture in January. Ed knew that Desolation Shoal was the best place to catch lobsters in winter and they would fetch a good market price. Few men ventured out this time of year, but you had to plan for the right tide and weather conditions. Four or five hours would be all they needed. At high tide the sea would cover Desolation Shoal making it especially dangerous, but they should be home long before supper with a boatload of lobsters to show for their efforts.

Ed checked the wind. It was from the east at about ten knots and the tide was right. Yes, a storm was predicted for nightfall, but they had plenty of time before it would be moving up the coast. An experienced mariner, he was always looking for sudden changes in the wind and the sea surface. Everything seemed perfect, but Ed kept a weather eye on the murk off his bow and a steady hand on the helm. The steady drumming of the engine was monotonous, but reassuring.

Billy checked on the fish heads that they would use to re-bait their traps after they were hauled on board. Umber, like an old fashioned figurehead, was stationed at the bow, wagging his tail and barking into the wind. Groping in his pock-

Louis Arthur Norton
West Simsbury, CT

et for his pipe, Ed suddenly discovered that he had left his tobacco at home. He frantically searched all his pockets and although he had matches, there was no tobacco. Somewhat irritated, Ed clamped his pipe between his teeth, and then sucked aimlessly on the empty pipe. He was superstitious like many who made their living on the sea. Ed worried, *Was this an omen?* They had a water jug and he had a stowed pint of whiskey in case it got too uncomfortable off the rocky island. In the cooler were lunches that Ed had prepared, so he felt reassured. Passing the headland he turned the lobster boat toward the open ocean. The wind was noticeably stronger off shore and the cold coming from the sea a bit more than he expected. Astern the headland faded into the distance, but no other boats were about. The lobster boat motored toward a foreboding belly of rock protruded from the sea, Desolation Shoal.

The Atlantic swelled and swirled as they hauled the first of the traps within sight of shore and made themselves as comfortable as they could out of the wind on the lee of the cockpit. The trip made both of them hungry, but they decided to wait and eat their sandwich after they had their catch stowed onboard. They did, however, give a snack to Umber. Despite the wind and cold, they were warm enough in their woolen clothes and socks underneath oilskins and knee-high rubber boots. Father and son continued to haul and re-bait their traps. Meanwhile the tide rose and the nearby rocky island started to disappear into the sea. The catch in the traps was good, but looking aloft the lobsterman was beginning to have misgivings. The wind freshened, shifted to the northeast and ominous dark storm clouds merged onto heavier solid forms and scudded toward them. The island's rocks suddenly turned dark like a liquid had recently been poured on them from the sea.

Overhead, white herring gulls with gray wings squawked loudly as they flew toward the shelter of the mainland. The choppy sea formed blankets of foam on its surface the

Louis Arthur Norton
West Simsbury, CT

residue of wind-driven surf. Ed thought that it was time that they headed home. He turned toward Billy, took his empty pipe from his mouth and started to speak when he caught sight of a moving blue-green wall of water.

A twenty-foot rogue wave raced toward them. It crashed into the starboard side of the *Katie M.*, almost capsizing them. The resulting turbulence threw the vessel onto the rocks of Desolate Shoal like a toy boat discarded by an unruly child. With a thunderous crack, the lobster boat's keel shattered and the vessel split into several pieces. The icy sea formed tentacles that reached into the broken hull carrying away their gear, water, whisky, the remaining food and their catch. *The Katie M.*, their lifeline, was now mostly scraps of flotsam. The ocean washed Desolation Shoal clean of anything that stood upon it except for the drenched Ed, Billy and Umber, castaways stranded on the rocky island.

Billy peered at the water in fear. Umber violently shook saltwater from his back, ran back and forth softly whining, and then sank to his belly, his muzzle on his forepaws. It was getting much colder.

"Damn it!" the lobsterman yelled as he sighted what was left of the their boat bobbing on the sea about fifty yards away.

"Dad," asked Billy, "what do we do now?"

"I might be able to swim to that large piece of the boat's hull, but that wouldn't do us any good." Ed gazed into the eyes of his son. "Besides the cold water is likely do me in."

"Let's wave something and shout. Somebody passing by might see or hear us," Billy replied in desperation.

Ed stared silently at the increasingly angry sea.

The rising water looked dark and foreboding as thickening clouds obscured the sun. Ed had told his wife that they would be home long before dark, but the daylight hours were pretty short during Maine winters. Seeing that they were not in by late afternoon, Kate would probably send neighbors to look for them right away. In good weather, it was an hour or so run to the lobster grounds off Desolation Shoal.

The intensifying storm and rising tide was rapidly shrinking the island's edges; their temporary earthen lifeboat was almost awash. The cold sea and the biting wind now bore a deathly chill. When a wave reached just below the lobsterman's booted knees he said to Billy, "Get up on my shoulders." The boy quickly obeyed. Ed opened his oilskin jacket and clamped Billy's booted ankles into his body with his elbows and, for added safety, tucked them under his stout workman's suspenders.

"What about Umber?" the boy asked.

Hearing his name, the dog looked at Billy and cocked an ear and barked.

"He'll be all right," Ed said. "He can take the cold water."

The wintry sea swept the island with a relentless ebb and flow. Suddenly the lobsterman's black rubber thigh-high boots filled with water. In a matter of minutes Ed's legs were numb and he began to shiver. While atop his father's shoulders, Billy's extended arms reached about nine feet above the drenched rocky ledge. Billy removed his yellow oilskin jacket and frantically waved it over his head and shouted. Just then a second huge wave engulfed the island. The powerful cascade mercilessly swept the three of them into the sea.

When Ed and Billy did not return for dinner, Kate franticly called her nearest neighbor. The word quickly spread to everyone in the tightly-knit community—an alert too often heard. Kate regretted that she had not joined them at breakfast this morning, guilt mingled with her worst fears.

At daybreak a fleet of small craft scurried off shore like swarming water bugs. By mid-morning they found the pieces of a lobster boat on the headland's rocks. Painted on a splintered stern-board was the name *Katie M.* Close by was the frozen form of a chocolate brown retriever. They frantically continued the search. At about noon the floating body of Ed Merrell was found. Kate, shortly thereafter, received a phone call from a neighbor asking her to come to the village's main

Louis Arthur Norton
West Simsbury, CT

wharf. Instinctively expecting the worst, Kate hesitated at first. Gaining courage, she climbed into their salt rusted pickup truck and drove over the snow-rutted roads to the village's waterfront.

The remaining lobstermen grimly continued to drag the depths for the boy, but were thus far unsuccessful. By late afternoon, one of the lobster boats brought Ed home. There was an eerie silence among those present as his body lay on the Snow Harbor Wharf. The lobsterman's dead eyes stared heavenward and his frozen arm clutched a rubber boot inside of which was an ice-encrusted red woolen sock. Kate stood transfixed. First she looked at the stiff body of her husband. One neighbor placed a hand tenderly on her arm as Kate looked out to the perilous sea that still held her Billy. The Atlantic Ocean had supported her family, but it also exacted a terrible price for giving this sustenance.

She shivered. Her frequent nightmare, no longer a predilection, had become a harsh horrible reality. If only she had said more before they left home yesterday morning. Even surrounded by friends, she felt alone. Overwhelmed at first, she did not know what to do.

She then saw her minister standing beside her husband's body. All who earned their living from the sea took comfort in the belief or hope that God looked after them. She put a finger to the corner of her eye, wiped away a tear, and then recited lines 23 through 26 of the 107th Psalm. Those on the dock standing near, their heads bowed, knew it well and joined her.

Louis Arthur Norton
West Simsbury, CT

They that go down to the sea in ships, that do business in great waters;

These see the works of the Lord, and his wonders in the deep.

For he commands, and raises the stormy wind, which lifts up the waves thereof.

They mount up to the heaven, they go down again to the depths: their soul is melted away because of trouble.

Their melancholy voices drifted out of Snow Harbor and onto the cruel sea.

Jim Mello
Farmington, ME

Awaiting Awakenings

in sacred Quaker space
the poetry tribe gathers
        to quicken metaphoric eyes
and hone haiku ears

outside/the white pine
needle by needle
        drinks in
February sun

its basking limbs
anchored by Christmas bulb cones
        dangling

the Ghost of holy silence lingers
where quieted hearts
        listened

for Spirit stirrings

in their turn, the poets
in unspoken prayer
        listen too

for divine breathings
        awakening images
slumbering in simmering embers

awaiting flamings
for fiery tongues

Veronica Kegel-Giglio
Philadelphia, PA

I Did Love You

Were you real, or did I just dream of you?
I held you so close that I could feel my own heart pick up a
beat as I held you
I confided my worst fears to you
I also told you about all my grandiose dreams and
ambitions
You listened never saying anything
I loved you because you heard me. Yet you did not judge
me
Nor did you criticize me
My parents did, but you did not
I told you about all the things I despised and hated
You listened to all
I remember us on the beach together and in the park
playing, singing, and laughing
Was that a dream?
Did I go crazy or just lose consciousness.
Maybe I just grew up too fast
Because now I am standing here holding you once again
and I can see
You are only a doll

Nancy B. Wilson
Bremen, ME

Come As You Are

You can
come as you are
when you come to the war
whatever you wear won't
matter at all
if you get to the front,
to the horror and gore
no one will notice whatever you wear,
so long as you're there.

But if
you can't get to the front,
live too far
just stay as you are
skyclad, or pj'd, even suited your best
for you don't want to miss
any gore, any horror—
you can relax by your TV
for a very good view,
else wait in your yard,
for it's not really hard
for war to come straight home to you.

Nancy B. Wilson
Bremen, ME

Only
the generals care what they wear
they won't come as they are, but
get dressed in full uniform, shine
their medals, for valor, all bright,
then they sit in their cosy armchairs
remote from the fight, from the horror and gore
where you are
knowing their outfit's just right
for the war.

But when
it's all over, this war
to end war,
and everyone's dead
(vain generals too—
what good did it do
them to care what they wore?)
from the horror and gore
it won't matter a bit
what you wore
it won't matter a whit
—when everyone's dead—
what anyone wore
to the war.

Mollie Schmidt
Rome, ME

Winter Wren

The liquid trill
of the winter wren
goes on and on—

how can this
small brown bird
send forth his long

intricate signal
morn to eve,
a spate of sound

delivered daily
from tiny throat
to astonished ears,

a language varied,
vehement, voice
of the troglodyte.

Maureen Anaya
Berwick, ME

Peppermint Patti

Tina, a five year old, entered the orphanage for girls assisted by an attendant, named Anne, whom took Tina's tiny hand and gently guided her down a long corridor to a room, which housed two girls. Louise, a seven year old, red-head, fair, with numerous facial freckles sat quietly watching an educational program, on the school's TV station, which was specially designed to instill educational values. Louise was engrossed with the program; therefore, barely noticed the two as they entered the room.

"Louise, this is your new roommate, Tina," Anne stated.

"Hi," Louise said. She turned quickly to acknowledge Tina, and then continued to watch the program.

Anne glanced at Tina and noticed how unkempt she looked: tangled, curly, dark hair partially covered her smooth olive face, which was streaked with dried tears. Her dress was tattered and slightly soiled. Tina's dark eyes looked up at Anne with admiration as she clutched an old worn rag doll. It was Tina's only possession since her parents died in an auto accident.

"And who is this?" Anne gestured towards the doll.

"Peppermint Patti," Tina's hoarse voice replied. "She goes everywhere with me."

"Well, we'll put the doll on your bed while you get washed up and ready for lunch," Anne suggested.

Reluctantly, Tina let Anne put the doll on her bed. Peppermint Patti was so named from the dress, which had red and white stripes (like a candy cane). Her brown yarn hair was parted in the middle with two pigtails down her back; loose ribbons held the pigtails in place. Peppermint Patti had a round face and a lovely smile. The doll was old and worn but Anne recognized the attachment Tina had to Peppermint Patti and she decided it would be unwise to part

Maureen Anaya
Berwick, ME

Tina with her doll.

Tina was not social with the other children and stayed in her room. She refused to eat.

Anne recently graduated from college. She was young and vibrant with an outgoing personality suited to her teaching ability with children; therefore, her decision to draw Tina out of her shell and see her become more social was a challenge.

One day Anne decided to try a new approach, since Tina had lost weight due to lack of nourishment. Anne, seeing Tina alone in her room holding the doll, brought in a luncheon plate. "Tina, you have to eat. If you don't, you'll be ill. Peppermint Patti wouldn't have anyone to care for her. She may be tossed out in the trash. You don't want that to happen?" Anne stated. To Anne's amazement Tina started to eat.

The orphanage started to host Family Nights and, after extensive background checks, place children in homes.

A couple, Mr. Jim Adams and his wife Vera arrived at the orphanage to view the children. On one of these occasions, they choose Louise. After a few visits, the couple decided she would fit in nicely with their family. Louise was overjoyed. She prepared to leave the orphanage one day and turned to Tina.

"Bye, Tina," Louise said.

When the Adams came into the room to remove Louise's belongings, they viewed Tina as she sat nearby: tears streaming down her face. Tina was losing Louise. The tiny fragile girl hugged Peppermint Patti.

"Vera," Mr. Adams addressed his wife. "The Stanley's daughter, Marge, died of cancer last year and she was the same age as Tina. They left Marge's room intact. I'm going to suggest they visit because something about this little girl reminds me of Marge."

Anne was very concerned about Tina after Louise left. Tina seemed to be losing more weight and withdrawing from social contact. Every day Anne spent some time with her.

Maureen Anaya
Berwick, ME

On Family Night, Joe and Barbara Stanley came to the orphanage to see Tina. Anne brought Tina out of her room and into the visitor's area; Tina clutched Peppermint Patti. The shy, sad Tina won their hearts and reminded them of their deceased daughter, Marge. They decided to make weekly visits and bring Tina cookies or toys to win her trust. She looked forward to their visits.

"We would like Tina to live with us," Mr. Stanley said to Anne one visit.

"I hope you can help her," Anne said.

"I believe we can. We'll only take her if she agrees to come with us."

Tina came into the room where weekly visits took place anticipating a special gift as usual. She was not disappointed when Barbara handed her a box of peanut butter cookies. Tina hugged the doll closely and sat near Barbara Stanley, opened the box of cookies, and started to eat one. Joe sat on the other side.

"Would you like to come and live with us?" Barbara asked.

"Can Peppermint Patti come, too?" Tina asked weakly.

"Yes," said Joe. "If you do decide to come live with us, there is a special room where Peppermint Patti will have several rag doll friends. She wouldn't be lonesome. Wouldn't you like her to have friends?"

"Really!" Tina's eyes lit up. "A whole room of rag dolls! Peppermint Patti would love it."

Within a month, Tina left the orphanage with the Stanleys. Anne was happy for Tina.

As promised, Tina entered her new room at the Stanley's home, where rag dolls sat in small chairs around a miniature table. Tina placed Peppermint Patti in an empty chair with the other dolls.

"Now you will have lots of friends to play with," Tina said to Peppermint Patti.

Emily B. Ellis
Lewiston, ME

The Yellow Fence

He'd say the color made him think of lemons
not too bright
not quite honey
just enough to make a claim of home
where at day's end
a destination

See them leaning on a picket
two boys
one just taller, hair more flaxen
stirring heavy metal bucket
paint lapping over side
other laughing
through his missing teeth
thumbs dangling from suspenders
sundried dandelions on kneecaps
eyes shadowing the easy grace of
movements
soaking in the fluid sweep of brush
upon old knobby knotty boards
awing wordlessly the tawny arm
whose strokes so vertical, so measured

the same arm on his shoulder
calming, healing
in those moments of wild sudden rage
when everyone a stranger—
except he
who taught him how to focus
on an image, object, memory
keep, where it cannot be stolen
ever

Emily Ellis
Lewiston, ME

here, this fence,
so many years, another time
when it was newly yellow
beacon in a muted starless night
its thick posts broken, pickets sagging
as his knees
still he's laughing
through more missing teeth
feels the arm draped round his shoulder
now,
forever.

***

Maude Olsen
South Bristol, ME

Neighbors

We live our lives with little thought
  To what occurs on yonder lot;
Our neighbors carry on their lives
  As other bees in other hives.

Across the way they come and go,
  Just where or why we cannot know
Unless we take the time to say,
  "How are you, friend, on this fine day?"

If we let them know we care
  They, too, may be more apt to share.

Dorothy Weiss
Orlando, FL

Terror in the Night

I was driving too fast! My eighty-year-old friend had just been admitted to the hospital after being dug out from the rubble of her tornado-destroyed home. I had been watching the news coverage of three tornadoes spinning through the central Florida area—Daytona, Winter Springs, and Kissimmee. I had friends in all three areas, and as the news reports came in, my concerns deepened and my calm went out the window. I had been trying to hold my worst fears at bay.

Upon arriving at the hospital, I parked my car askew, jumped out and ran down the corridor and into my friend's room. She reached for me babbling, "I was watching the storm warning on television, sitting in my easy chair near my living room windows. Suddenly, I heard a voice command: "MOVE!" I ran to a closet. The next thing I heard was a roar and whistle like a train bearing down on me. Instantly, I was buried up to my neck in debris, unable to move. In the rain and darkness, I kept screaming, "Help me, help me!" Then a soft blue light and a gently humming sound appeared and stayed with me until the rescuers found me and pulled me free. I wouldn't ever want to experience another tornado, but that light and sound was beautiful. My fear just melted away. You believe me, don't you?" she pleaded. "Has anything like that ever happened to you?"

Astonished by her words, all I could do was hug her and whisper, "I believe you." I had read about people having near death experiences and seeing or hearing things beyond the realm of the physical senses. But here was my dear friend telling me something she encountered and whatever it was had helped her survive until rescuers freed her from the debris under which she was trapped. She was alive, with minor scratches and bruises, but otherwise unhurt. I held

Dorothy Weiss
Orlando, FL

her gently, kissed her forehead, and repeated, "I believe you."

That was seven years ago. Through the years people told her that her experience was a result of the shock she suffered from that horrific tornado. Just hallucinating, they said, but she clung steadfast to what she saw and heard. "No, it was real!" She would declare.

Socrates, Plato, Theresa of Avila, St. Francis of Assisi and countless other sages and beings in history alluded to experiencing mystical beautiful light and sounds. As a child I has listened with wonder to those ancient stories my parents told me about Saul of Tarsus on the road to Damascus stopped by light and a voice commanding him to return to Rome to help the early Christians being persecuted; and then there was Moses and the light and voice within a burning bush that did not burn. Now here in the present was a person I couldn't dismiss or ignore, who fully accepted her experience as a spiritual moment, an encounter to be cherished forever.

She died last year. I remember her and whisper still, "I believe you."

Jean Lawrence
Waldoboro, ME

Observe, People of Waldoboro

The many ways our town has grown.
Stahl and Miller tell of the migrants to Broad Bay.
They found no waiting "Welcome" no planned growth
    pattern,
only wilderness and river.
Look through history's few recorded lines.
See the steady progression of life
up the Dutch Man's Neck and the river's east shore to the
    three falls.
See where broad farms flourished and ferries traversed the
    river.
View the site where village life took root, where fledgling
    yards like seeds sprouted.
Dissension, patriotism, scandal, and creativity:
All existed side by side.
Over time, influenced and fed were these needs:
    to become independent, to incorporate, to mature,
    to become our town, our home.
What will we add to the town's future?
What will we write in our chapter of Waldoboro's
    development?

Kathryn Warren
Westfield, NJ

Nick

I cried deeply today. It all started with a telephone call to dear Nick....Today is Nick's 95th birthday. Although this may seem incredible, it really isn't. Ninety-five is simply Nick's age; it's just a number. To hear Nick speak, you'd think he were no older than a very young seventy. Despite the fact that Nick may no longer have a spring in his step, there's much life and magic in his voice. Nick is truly a treasure.

Everyone has friends. Some are childhood friends and others come to us during different stages of our lives. Then there are those extraordinary friends who are more like relatives than the ones we have. Nick Rivaldo was my father's dearest friend. He was Dad's card-playing buddy, and the one he shared many a glance or subtle nod with from across a club house table during their cherished and frequent card games. I never knew much about those card games. Dad hardly talked about them. There were times I'd be visiting my parents and see firsthand my father's twice a week ritual of driving two short blocks to the clubhouse where he'd meet the guys and their night of card playing would begin. It was only after Dad was gone that I'd come to know some of the subtle signals passed between my dad and Nick during those games—stories now shared in precious phone conversations I now have with Nick. Yes, whenever we speak, Nick tells me story after story about him and my dad, but mostly about my dad. It's these very conversations and Nick's endearing words that always hit me the hardest. Not surprisingly, tonight's exchange went straight to the heart.

Nick was Dad's Florida friend and that's really all I ever knew about him. Nick was the one person Dad would always connect with during those cold New York winters he and Mom warmly spent in their Tamarac home. My father was

Kathryn Warren
Westfield, NJ

the youngest of three brothers, and I'm sure they were as close as brothers can be, but in Dad's later years, Nick was it. These two gentlemen bonded in a way I've never seen before. They'd laugh together and talk at length, not just about who'd won the previous night's hand, but about so many other things that showed a level of comfort and intelligence undoubtedly savored by each.

My parents used to call New York home and Florida their winter getaway. Eventually, Florida became their year-round residence and Nick became Dad's year-round friend. Compelled to sell their home in Ozone Park and move to Florida meant frequent visits to my family here in New Jersey. It was during these visits that Dad would be sure to give Nick a call to see how he was doing. My father was not a telephone person; it just wasn't in his nature to call anyone and have lengthy conversations or just shoot the breeze. But with Nick it was different; he'd always call Nick. I remember one call, in particular, when Dad was told that Nick's beloved wife had passed away. The sadness in Dad's voice and on his face was palpable. It didn't matter that Dad hardly knew her. This was personal. This was about Nick.

Then there were those other conversations with Nick that I was often so privileged to witness, conversations that always lifted my father's spirits. I can still hear the lilt in my father's voice as Nick would pick up the phone on the other end. *"Hello, Nick,"* he'd say, as if singing the opening lyric of a familiar song; and their telephone visit across the miles would begin, always ending with my dad asking about the *boys*—yes, there were other card-playing friends, too. As he'd ask about their latest card game, I always knew Dad wished he was there. I relished hearing my father's laughter as he'd listen intently to Nick sharing the antics of each of the guys. No doubt, these same stories had been shared before, but were stories that always seemed new again and embraced by my dad. As a bystander of these lively conversations, it was wonderful to see these special *visits* take place between my

Kathryn Warren
Westfield, NJ

dad and his faithful friend. I think I always knew my father enjoyed playing poker and black jack with his buddies, but it wasn't until his final weeks with us, when I became immersed in his world, that I truly understood his love for his buddy Nick.

It was during my father's final days that I came to know and love Nick. After Dad's surgeries that summer, his days and weeks were spent in a rehabilitation facility. Dad's spirits were often low during these difficult times and he was not always in the mood for visitors. Nevertheless, he'd greet everyone who walked through the door with such love and appreciation, no matter what kind of a day he was having. Fortunately for me, I was at Dad's side constantly and knew when his cheerful greetings were contrived or genuine. With Nick, they were always heartfelt. All it would take was a surprise visit from Nick to see Dad's demeanor instantly change. Immediately, there'd be a smile on my dad's face and laughter in the air. It didn't matter that I'd just spent the entire day at his side, a part of which was spent playing our own game of cards that I certainly knew neither of us was enjoying. I simply wasn't one of the guys. No, none of that could add a glimmer to Dad's day as much as a visit from his buddy Nick. Now that I think about it, I was always delighted to see Nick, too. Those afternoons when Nick would pop in for a visit were pure magic.

Naturally, I think of Nick often and I sometimes call him. I call Nick only when I feel emotionally strong. I call because I want to know he's alright. I want to know he's still there, and with every call I am reminded yet again that my father isn't. I call because I love hearing his voice—my father's voice is silent. However, it's during conversations like tonight's that I simply fall apart. Nick is not my father. I know that. My father can never be replaced. But when I hear Nick speak with such affection about my dad and all that they shared, my father is right there with him—with us. Nick's words are always eloquent and filled with love, but for some reason

Kathryn Warren
Westfield, NJ

tonight my father was a part of him. As he called me *sweetheart*, I could hear my father's voice. Did he even know that my father always called me his sweetheart? And as he spoke of wanting to hug me through the phone, I melted and felt my father's arms.

People enter our lives for so many reasons. As we ended tonight's conversation with me wishing Nick the happiest of birthdays, I silently thanked my father. Nick is in my life because of him. In my heart, I truly believe that Nick is here to continue to give me one of life's greatest gifts—a father's love.

GOOSE RIVER ANTHOLOGY, 2012

We seek selections of fine poetry, essays, and short stories (3,000 words or less) for the 10th annual *Goose River Anthology, 2012*. Book will be beautifully produced with full color cover and hard covers will have a full color dust jacket.

You may submit even if you have been published before in a previous edition of the *GRA*. We retain one-time publishing rights. All rights revert back to the author after publication. You may submit as many pieces as you like.

EARN CASH ROYALTIES. Author will receive a 10% royalty on all sales that he or she generates.

There is no purchase required and nothing is required of the author for publication. Deadline for submissions is April 30, 2012. Publication will be in the summer of 2012. (they make great Christmas gifts). Guidelines are as follows:

- Submit clean, typed copy
- Reading fee: $1.00 per page
- Do not put two poems on the same page
- Essays and short stories should be double-spaced
- SASE for notification (.44 cents) plus additional postage for possible return of submission if desired
- Author's name & address at top of each page

Submit to:
Goose River Anthology, 2012
3400 Friendship Road
Waldoboro, ME 04572-6337
Telephone: (207) 832-6665
E mail: gooseriverpress@roadrunner.com
www.gooseriverpress.com

www.ingramcontent.com/pod-product-compliance
Lightning Source LLC
Chambersburg PA
CBHW020551310726
48979CB00008B/1178/J